Squeal

GITTE TAMAR

BTW LLC

OINK
OINK
OINK

To those who blame others for their sorrow, never
be expectant of apology or change; that will only
feed the narcissistic beast involved in the trivial
game, and likely, you will be engrossed in shame;
instead, try flipping the narrative and moving on;
only then will the trauma soon be gone.

HAPPY
FAMILY

Thank you

WARNING:
This story includes situations of violence, gore,
death, abuse, implied sexual situations/assault,
and swear or curse words.

Contents

Chapter One

WHO IS HUNGRY?

1977, Bellmore, Ohio

For an outsider looking in, the farmland appears peaceful, but things are not always what they seem.

Evil is a tiny seed planted deep in our guts at birth, and it flourishes when one allows wickedness to consume their heart. Though we have been taught to be ashamed of evil thoughts and deeds, everyone is born with the groundwork to fall into their malignancy, and it is a fine line that separates whether the individual answers the evil's call.

Our fate lies in our resiliency, our desire to live. There are moments when a simple choice can determine our destiny. It is a bit like a lottery—some will win, and some will lose.

For dear Tom, one dreary night, he wins the jackpot.

The evening starts quite typically, with twinkling stars in the clear sky above a characteristic farmstead raising pigs. Inside the barn's tin structure, a light on the verge of burning out pulsates from bright to dim. From a distance, the design mimics the appearance of a jack-o'-lantern as the light flickers through the milky fiberglass windows.

This is not an everyday occurrence. Usually, by nightfall, the chores are complete, and the barn is locked, with lights extinguished for the day, but tonight, something is different. The consistent reality has changed.

The crickets chirp loudly outside, masking the scene's abnormality, with each small voice creating a split-octave harmony that resonates through the crisp night air. Adjacent to the flickering structure is an old two-story farmhouse, and hidden on the backside of its green trim is a form of chaos no one would anticipate.

Behind the ragged screen door entrance is a rickety staircase with worn steps. The creaky steps lead to the second floor, and the home's only bathroom.

Inside the tiny space, a buzzing bulb illuminates the room's small window facing the barn, and what is transpiring inside the four walls would raise the hair on the back of one's neck. The standard routine of brushing his teeth has been replaced by a horrific scene that will forever change an eighteen-year-old's existence.

This is when a freshly legal-aged man's life ends—or, as he would argue, begins.

The small room swirls with immense anxiety as heavy heart palpitations mimic an off-tempo bass drum booming within the four confining walls. The sound is so suffocating that he cannot identify its origin.

Feeling overwhelmed, he races to the oblong vanity mirror to gather his thoughts. He gazes dead-on at his reflection and refuses to look down. His complexion is void of color.

The tightening of his lungs tells him something external isn't causing the unrelenting noise; it is resonating from inside his chest, and the chirping insects outside challenge his racing heart to match the tempo of their melodic tune.

In a futile attempt to slow his breathing, he focuses on the whites of his irises and observes bloodshot veins spreading like a virus across his eyes. Every fresh worry causes his pupils to dilate and his panic to grow.

Refusing to break his stare, he forces his breathing to slow, and his jaw clenches to spew fictitious affirmations. "You can do it, Tom. Come on," he says as his eyes dart to the side of the mirror's beveled glass edges.

The delicate tan vines, light green leaves, and pastel-pink roses that adorn the wallpaper covering the walls catch his attention, triggering memories he would rather forget. Each decorative element is slightly raised above the forest-green background, adding texture to the touch.

Never having liked the floral scenes' misrepresentation, the sight of the vines with no prickly thorns torments his mind. His loathing over the false depiction escalates, triggering thoughts of a more challenging time when he was plucked from his childhood home and thrown into the foster care system.

Through his heartbreaking adolescence, he could never understand why his grandparents had abandoned him for years before magically deciding to be his savior. He constantly asked himself why they did not choose to rescue him when seeing the pure neglect inflicted on him by his parents and subsequent foster homes. Each time a substitute family returned him to the foster system, he felt unworthy of love. His resentment for his grandparents grew with every rejection, and his respect for them diminished.

Not once did he consider that poor finances could be the reason for their decision to let others take him in, or that they wanted him to have a better life that they couldn't monetarily provide. Instead, he only fixated on the negative impact their decisions selfishly put upon him. As he moved on from each dysfunctional temporary home, he would fantasize about how he might evoke revenge for their desertion.

By the time the elderly couple raised enough money through farming to provide him with a roof over his head and food to eat, it was too late for his opinion to change. The day he moved in with his grandparents, he didn't consider the hard work and sacrifice required to create the opportunity; instead, through his rose-colored glasses, he only saw their possessions and the life they'd deprived him of.

In anticipation of his arrival, they'd spruced up his new room with fresh linens and remodeled the upstairs bathroom to make his new home more comfortable. The only thing left to finish was choosing the decor for the restroom walls. They'd asked for his opinion to make Tom feel included, and with a sense of entitlement, he'd expressed his view. He had been livid when his grandfather returned from town with a heinous vine wallpaper chosen by his grandmother.

They genuinely didn't know him and overlooked the frustration, not realizing that his hatred ran deep, festering like necrosis under his skin. They believed installing it as a family would be fun and that his anger would subside. Tom found no silver lining in the endeavor, and deemed them making him install it as a cruel punishment.

Being forced to look at the mocking flowers again triggers the memory of their selfishness and makes his blood boil. To calm his anger, he methodically counts each pink rose. "One, two, three, four..."

As his voice quickens, his thoughts spiral deeper into a darkened place, and his vision blurs. Finding his usual attempt not working, he becomes desperate and fumbles through his mind for validation. As he tries to convince himself, the skin on his face becomes clammy. "This isn't you."

The words cause his hands to convulse with tremors. Worried about what he will do next, he blindly reaches for the bathroom faucet. With a single twist of the handle, the hot water streams into the white porcelain bowl, and steam rises in the air, fogging his reflection.

While looking in the mirror, his image becomes slightly fuzzed, giving him the appearance of an apparition. Enjoying the moment of anonymity, he turns the handle further, causing steam to boil up from the scalding water hitting the bowl. It oddly comforts him and reminds him of when he uses the garden hose to cool off the pigs on hot summer days. The water hitting their torsos sounded like fingers tapping on drums while steam rose from cooling their warm bodies, and they always showed their appreciation with happy oinks.

The warm moist heat from the building condensation infiltrates his eyes and thrusts his dream back to reality. He stares, wide-eyed, at the irritated whites of his eyes. "You are a mess-up, just like everyone thought you were." Each hateful word cuts through the haze like a viper's hiss.

Wanting to escape the harsh criticism, his eyes tightly shut, and his hands shake with turmoil and sadness. Through his confusion, he tries to tame them and, unable to do so, gives in to defeat.

His heart seethes with self-loathing over what has transpired, and that he has allowed the darkness in his mind to take control of his actions.

His convulsing hands answer the call of the sloshing heat and move in the direction of the running water. His lungs expand freely, contradicting his body's tension by taking a deep breath, and his mouth calmly speaks. "Everything is fine. You are fine."

The water's noise grows louder in his ears as the oncoming steam builds a thicker fog around his cheeks. Still having yet to feel any pain from the faucet's scorching stream, he becomes confused. His eyelids dart open to investigate why, and he realizes that his hands are still an inch away from the tap, getting only a taste of the enthralling baking sensation that's to come.

This is the first time he is forced to acknowledge his fists, and his pupils lock on them with horror. They are drenched in a heavy coating of dark crimson. The thick consistency has turned translucent from the boiling mist, causing diluted pink-hued droplets to color the porcelain below.

In addition to the visual, he discerns the stench of heavy iron being carried by the up-moving condensation. As it flows into his nostrils, he connects the dots, confirming his suspicion that the substance is blood. He flips his hands over to analyze the scarlet-tainted dirt underneath his rough, ridged fingernails. Taking in a deeper whiff of the aroma, he waits for the recollection of how it got on his skin to come back to his mind, but his memory is blank.

The water's boiling heat continues to climb, forming a whistling in the pipes.

His teeth grit together to stop his deadening thoughts, and, wanting to feel something, he stares at his reflection again. A pair of soulless eyes glare back at him. Convinced, he spots an emerging smirk on his reflection's face. He shouts, "Do you think this is funny?"

As he peers at himself, a deep sense of profound loathing takes over, and, repulsed, he exacts punishment by shoving his hands under the searing stream of water. The excruciating pain causes a chilling scream to exit his lungs. In agony, he glances toward the cracked ceiling to speak to the angels. "You happy now?"

Hearing no response, his harsh gaze returns to the mirror. This time, he notices the reflection of the small bay window carved into the bathroom wall behind him. Memories of the events gain traction in his mind as the self-inflicted torture continues to boil his skin. As he relishes the immense ache, he squints, and his mouth's corner creases bend to a sickening grin.

Outside the thin single-pane window, a scattering of stars surrounds a yellow half-crescent moon. Their luminescence reveals the secret he is trying to suppress. In the property's single barn, which is falling apart, barely held together by rusting nails through the structure's red tin paneled siding, resides a swarm of pigs squealing with hunger.

He finds the visual like a metaphor for the chaos swirling in his mind, and the sound of crying pigs makes him, for a split-second, return to his happy place. His nostrils flare as he senses the caressing sensation of the warm, humid air against his cheeks, and he imagines it filtering through the characteristic cracks of the foul-smelling barn.

Believing the creatures to be the only ones to accept him unconditionally, the sounds of the animals' pleading cries growing louder in his ears lure his repressed emotions to the surface, and his face turns red with a recollection of the horrific events.

The scent of cooking flesh joins the iron-filled aroma and snaps him back to the moment, cutting through the obstinacy of his drifting mind. It reeks like a home-cooked meal to his nauseous stomach. The tremendous pain causes his nervous system to disengage, normalizing the agony as he frantically tries to spin the narrative. "You are not the bad guy... You were only trying to protect them. *He* wanted to hurt them."

Thoughts of his nearest and dearest being harmed cause his blistered fists to clench under the searing stream. Knowing he saved them strengthens his smile, but the joy is short-lived.

Chaos ensues as the varying water pressure causes the old iron pipes' burden to increase. Noises of the sows' murderous cries echo against the bathroom's cream-colored tiling, and adding to the stress, the crickets' calls' pitches intensi-fy. Without warning, the shrills cause the single dome-light fixture on the ceiling to flicker like a strobe.

As if the clashing sounds weren't enough to over-whelm his fragile mind, the addition of the un-stable light makes it impossible for him to focus his thoughts, and the combined chaos fills him with rage. Pushed to his wit's end, the unbearable noise and agitation break him, and he succumbs to the pressure. Bursting with emotion, he loses control, and his fists strike the mirror's reflection in a rebellion.

The sound of the shattering glass causes him to freeze. As his mind takes a moment to find clarity, he analyzes the wounds on his fists. Watch-ing the trickling blood land in the sink fascinates him. Glancing up, he snickers with pleasure at the red smears of coagulating body matter left in the mirror's cracks. The colorful visual temporarily provides a blissful silver lining to his predicament.

Glass shards continue to tumble to the floor, and as they land, they break into tinier pieces against the tiling. He finds the sound unpleasant but is suddenly intrigued when a disturbing thought comes to mind. He scans his right foot, which is covered in heavy calluses and mud. Lifting it above the sharp accumulation of mirror fragments, his mind falls into autopilot, guiding his bare foot to hover an inch above the floor.

The view of the impending sharp edges agonizingly consumes him, causing his tears to spill over into his lower lids and pool them with water. He tenses his body, forcing it to break through his lungs' hyperventilation to speak. "I told him not to touch Olive."

Suddenly, he notices a new haunting tune mixed in with the echoes of chaos. It is the lingering sound of a grown man's bloodcurdling screams. He cannot make it stop. Falling into a worsening state of panic, he agitatedly moans, "Why did he choose to die? Why?"

Looking at his hovering foot, he gradually lowers the flat bottom of the sole to the heap of splintered glass. Without flinching, he shifts the total weight of his body onto the sharp points and watches as blood pools beneath his toes. The act of self-mutilation is healing to him, and the sight of the red liquid is grounding.

As he takes a deep breath, the voices untangle inside his mind, and his thoughts clear. Unable to see through the dense fog, he fumbles for the faucet to turn it off, and the excruciating pain of his skin's contact with the handle reminds him of his severe burns.

Silence sets over the room, and the pulsing light highlights the shelves of the medicine cabinet's interior between the remaining slivers of the bloody mirror. Frantically, he reaches through the shards and fumbles through the contents to find bandages. "What did you do, Tom?" he whispers. "What did you do?"

Seizing a spool of white gauze, he swiftly wraps his hands to stop the bleeding, then bandages his foot. He carefully moves toward the bathroom door while glancing at the floor to avoid stepping on fragments of broken glass. Not wanting to provoke his open blisters, he uses his wrists to twist the doorknob.

Before exiting, he takes one last glance toward the window. The sounds of the crickets chirping outside mask the truth by providing a false serenity. Even the barn's glimmering light plays upon the tranquility by slyly luring his attention in hopes of provoking his curiosity.

The calculated effort is unnerving, and the situation causes his body to shudder and his head to pivot away from the window, hiding the sight from view. "You will not be why I get locked up. I will make damn sure of that!" He says.

He takes a deep breath and steps out into the hall, leaving the bathroom mess behind. The change of scenery brings him peace, and without looking back, he slams the door shut to focus solely on the new environment surrounding him.

The hallway exudes the home's simplistic architectural design, with only two doors down the hall to the right past the washroom, each leading to one of the tiny house's only bedrooms. If one chooses to go to the left, there is a set of worn stairs; every single wooden tread is chipped and varies in color from extensive wear and lack of upkeep. In addition, the off-white painted walls are scuffed from moving furniture from the first floor to the second.

In a poor attempt to hide the marks, photos cover the most prominent abrasions. The family pictures lining the walls are organized to show the progression of their relationship. Having none from Tom's childhood to pull from, they hung an assortment of crayon drawings he made after his return, each portraying a different hog from the farm.

When they displayed the portraits, they believed they could better connect with their estranged grandchild by demonstrating support for his artistic interests. Unfortunately, just like the wallpaper, this was not the case; it did the opposite—it added to his sorrow. Thinking the pictures were endearing, they overlooked his inspiration for producing the artwork and the trauma that may have triggered the creativity.

Each of the depictions is not of a random animal. Through Tom's eyes, they have a greater purpose. They memorialize every swine he had grown attached to during his short-lived adolescence on the farm, and every stroke of his pen captured their victimization. Even though all the animals happily differ in characteristics or details, they share one commonality—each was butchered behind his back, sold for cash, and replaced with another to keep the farm in operation.

Over time, as the collection of paintings grew, the somber pictorial walk to his room became more burdensome. He was plagued by vivid nightmares of the piercing sets of black crayon-colored eyes, and he worried that the traumatic visions would come to fruition. Finally, his angst became so overwhelming that he diverted his gaze to the floor when passing their pictures on his nightly walk to bed. While in the privacy of his room, he spent countless nights crying himself to sleep over the loss of each companion.

Today is different; he feels free of guilt, and knowing the cycle of their mistreatment is over, he is comfortable staring all his friends directly in the dead center of each pupil.

The sounds of tiny snorts echo through his eardrums as he observes joy exuding from their crudely drawn depictions. It is clear they are celebrating him and cheering on a new beginning. He feels like he can read their minds. "You are free, my friends; no one will ever hurt you again, and that is a promise," he says.

Taking his time to reflect on their lives, he moves around the hall, acknowledging each one. Upon his final pass, he leans over and kisses every snout in the lineup to show his unwavering loyalty. During the last peck of his lips, an uncomfortable sound jolts him to an abrupt stop. It is the noise of a teakettle screeching a whistle from the kitchen.

As his ears ring, his throat releases a low, guttural cry. After the intense episode in the bathroom, he is at his wit's end and has no patience for the alarming shrill. Knowing he must make it stop, he instantly changes his trajectory, but upon his first step toward the staircase, a stabbing pain radiates from the torn skin on the bottom of his foot. The agony makes him lightheaded, his vision blurs, and his face loses all color as he fights back the urge to vomit.

Ignoring the discomfort, he reaches the top step. He glances down at the floor in response to the debilitating sensation and observes blood seeping through the bandage around his foot. The sight fuels his bullheaded nature, and he forces himself to fight through the agony in response. Trying to ease his suffering, his hand squeezes the unstable railing for support, and he uses it to assist him down each step, his jaw clenching tightly to mitigate the pain from his self-inflicted wounds.

As he descends, he scans the scenery below and realizes that every light is off except the kitchens on the lower level of the modest dwelling. Adjacent to the bottom step is a small dividing wall coated with off-white popcorn-styled plaster. It was installed to provide a bit of room separation between the living room and kitchen in the first floor's open layout.

Making the most of the small farmhouse's space restriction, the kitchen has an improvised dining table pushed against the wall to allow seating for three. Off to the right of the staircase is a tiny living room with two worn brown-leather couches and a braided-rag rug in rust-red and mustard-yellow hues.

Ignoring the pitch-black space to his right, he focuses on the light shining from the direction of the kitchen. As he gets further down the steps, he winces. The crying teapot grows louder in his ears, and he glares at the warm light shining around the off-white dissecting partition. "How many times do I have to remind that woman to turn that damn thing off?" he says as he covers his ears with his bandaged hands. His molars grit against each other to combat his annoyance, and he continues down the steps with a deep breath.

The whistling continues, and he wonders why no one is addressing the deafening sound. Unsure what he may find, his blistered fists squeeze at his sides as if preparing to fight. He cautiously approaches and, upon reaching the shallow wall, peeks around the corner to look.

The familiar sight causes him to chuckle with a sigh of relief. "Oh, am I glad to see it's you! I was worried I would have to deal with an intruder," he says as his fists relax.

His grandmother's body lies motionless on the kitchen floor near the dining room table, surrounded by a sizable pool of blood. Crimson fluid continues to seep from her fresh wounds, trickling in small streams between the grooves of the floorboards.

Delighted by his discovery, he wipes his perspiring forehead with his hand's bandage and steps inside the room to join her. The patterns of blood resemble abstract art to him. Fascinated by the progression of the carnage, he tilts his head to assess the burgundy exhibition.

Curlers with spooled gray hair fell victim to her fate and now reside in the concave sections of her profoundly bludgeoned skull. Coagulating sludge leaks from her misshapen head and joins the thickening pool of blood. The signs of brutality continue to her torso, where innumerable stab wounds penetrate through the flannel material of her green-patterned nightgown. Her slippers lie several feet away from her body, making it clear she put up a struggle. Each shoe's knitted fabric is face-down, soaking up the liquid of the slowly spreading gore.

There is no mystery regarding the tool used to aid in her demise. A bloody butcher knife protrudes from her chest like a victory flag.

Disregarding the state of her mutilated appearance, his uncaring eyes immediately dart to the taunting kettle whistling on the stove. "Shut up!" he yells as he lividly limps in its direction. Using the countertops and walls for assistance, he continues his mission. "You be quiet."

He finds the obstacle of his grandmother's carnal mess inconvenient to step over, and with a dramatic roll of his eyes, he grunts to ease his frustration. Standing in front of the stove, he creatively uses the flats of his wrists to jimmy the knob of the gas burner. As he gets the dial to finish twisting, he hears something rustling behind him and, flinching, his elbow brushes against the teakettle. "Son of a bitch!" he shouts as he retracts his arm in pain.

Clutching the damaged skin, he turns toward the body sprawled on the ground to take out his outrage. "I'm sure you think this is funny, don't you?" he says.

His yell provokes the woman's slashed chest to rise slightly, and the movement causes a gurgling sound from her lungs. The notion of her still being alive intrigues him, almost like conducting a scientific experiment. "I always knew you were related to a cockroach," he says with a smirk.

Unsure of what is happening, in a plea for help, she musters up enough strength to shift her head toward the stove's noise and tries to speak. "H... help."

Still stewing over the accidental burn on his elbow, he is disgusted by her speech pattern and appearance; his pitch-black eyes show no pity for the woman. Pinning the blame for his misfortune on her lack of willingness to die, he moves his burning glare and hatefully stares directly into her pupils. "You see what you made me do?" he says as he lifts his bandaged hands and foot. "Do you?"

Unable to respond, her fingers lightly twitch, and with a gurgle, she tries again to speak. "H... help," she says.

Her pathetic attempt causes his head to shake with laughter. "You are useless," he says. Having had enough with her, he throws his hands into the air and begins to converse with himself, "I always knew you never cared about me."

His words deepen his contempt and his pent-up feelings of abandonment transfer from his gut to his face. His eyes well up as he fights back the tears. To bolster his pain, he clenches his fists, turning his sadness into a rage. "It was all a lie!" He points to her and yells, "You never loved me! People don't abandon those they love!"

Watching him, her eyelids stay plastered open as she silently fights to survive.

He wants her to experience his festering anguish and believes that her torture thus far does not adequately compare to the pain of his childhood. In a swift movement, he grabs the teapot. "Maybe it's time I give you a little taste of the suffering you caused me," he says as he creeps toward her. She cannot move and is disturbingly forced to watch every inch of his unhurried approach.

Upon reaching her body, he stands over her. "You thought you could get rid of me when I turned eighteen, didn't you? I'm not just another animal you pretend to love, then discard for slaughter. You are pure evil; I can see it in your eyes. We were family, but you ruined it, just like everything else," he says. His face fills with cynical rage as he reminisces on what could have been.

Running out of time, her throat gurgles, and her lungs spew more blood.

"Coward," he says with a shaking head. "That's what you are—just a coward." The insult causes him to grin.

Enjoying watching her suffer, he lifts his hand with the kettle and delicately trickles the boiling water over her fidgeting fingers. The agony causes her to groan.

Her helplessness gives him a sick sense of pleasure; he mocks her with a sadistic grin as her life hangs by a thread. For once, he feels in control, and with the slightest movement, he sprinkles the scalding water into the deep gashes on her torso. Her moaning grows louder and resonates like a growl from her chest.

He cackles as he lifts the kettle's spout to stop the pour. "Don't worry. It will be over soon," he says. Sarcastically shrugging, he attempts to make peace with her. "I thought we could have worked things out. That was until I learned from good ol' grandpa that you expected me to move out when I turned eighteen." His confession causes him to relive the triggering conversation he had with his grandfather earlier that day while cleaning out the pig pens before dinner—Goosebumps form on his upper arms as his fears of being abandoned flood back. "You can't leave now; no one can. I hate to be the bearer of bad news, but you are stuck with me."

Her pitiful gaze stares in horror at the moving tea kettle over her head.

With a warm smile, he tilts his wrist to pour the rest of the scalding water over her face. He watches with amusement as her eyes cook from the heat and her skin blisters down to the muscle. Then, having nothing left to empty, he releases the metal pot from his hand to tumble on the floor. The heavy metal crashing against the wood is music to his ears, deepening his grin with a sense of accomplishment.

"Now, what do you say we go join that husband of yours?" He grabs her arms and uses his determination to drag her body toward the front door.

Barely holding on to consciousness, she remains limp as her vision turns black.

He finds lugging the dead weight of her frame through the dimly lit house a chore, and he fights through the effort by pulling harder on her limbs to pick up speed. Reaching the front door, he flings open the flimsy wooden barrier and, with a single tug, pulls her outside onto the dirt path. Taking a moment to catch his breath, he gazes at the beautiful scene in the sky above.

The shimmering stars reflect off the night sky's blue and black tones. Scattered about the farm's isolation, crickets chirp whimsical tunes from their refuges in the clusters of assorted tall grass filling the surrounding acreage. A light breeze blows, rustling the trees and pushing the manure odor from the barn toward the house.

Hearing the commotion, the pigs' plea louder for attention, and their high-pitched calls cut through the peaceful serenity.

Tom finds their cries concerning, and, not wanting to be the reason for their disappointment, he shortens his rest period. Knowing the property like the back of his hand, he travels backward, picking up his pace, remorselessly heaving his grandmother's body down the dusty path toward the red tin structure.

The squeals grow louder and drown out the happy chirps of the insects.

Wishing the awaiting barn residents would quiet down, Tom shouts over his shoulder to reassure them he is on his way. "Don't worry, I'm almost there!" he calls.

The residual echoes of his familiar voice through the open field cause the swine's squealing to escalate, but this time, their cries are different; they are filled with elation over his approach. Their exhilaration makes him smile, and a tear of acceptance forms in the corner of his eye.

As Tom, with the body in tow, closes in on the barn, the flickering light lets out an electrical buzz, signaling it is close to burning out, and the noise agitates him. Dropping his grasp on her arms, he uses all his body weight to push against the tin building's heavy sliding door, and the ungreased tracks let out a shriek.

Upon opening the entrance, he takes a moment to admire the familiarity of the structure's interior. His lungs take a deep inhale to revel in the moment of his happiness. He closes his eyes and lifts his bandaged hands to the height of his shoulders. Then, taking a long supporting breath, he gathers enough air to join in with his cloven-hooved family, and his nose loudly oinks to communicate.

They rambunctiously respond to the call by escalating the level of their grunts.

Feeding off their enthusiasm, he slowly looks back at his grandmother's disfigured body, and without an ounce of emotion, he charges her. "All right, time to go," he says as he grabs her ankles. The flickering barn light reflects off her matte irises as she drags across the concrete floor.

They make their way to the large pen, and he gazes with a grin at the metal fence housing the swarming pigs.

Bloodstains cover the bristles underneath their light pink wet snouts; it is almost as if clown-like crimson smiles have been painted on their lips.

Tom's eyes glance past the lively group to the stray bloody pitchfork behind them. "Who's ready for round two?" he asks with enthusiasm.

Their squeals grow louder in response.

Without wasting another moment, he picks her body up from the floor, hoists it over his shoulder, and, after bracing himself, carries her to the pen. As he stands in front of the paneled confines, he takes a moment to build their anticipation for the oncoming feast. Then, with a loud grunt, he thrusts her body over the fence with a mighty heave.

As the heavy thud of her dead weight hitting the dirt echoes between the walls, the pigs ravenously congregate around her like swarming bees.

Hearing the sound of her bones crushing between their flat teeth prompts Tom's eyes to shift to the bloodstained prongs protruding from the dirt. The cries of the squealing pigs soothe him, and he gleefully closes his eyes with a soft grin, reliving the memory of his grandfather's demise.

Chapter Two
CRUNCHING

Two Hours Earlier, The Barn

Even though the sky is darkening from the setting sun, the heat continues warming the tin structure's interior, making the environment almost unbearable to work in. The pen smells like a broken sewer line as the heat bakes the muddy mix of dirt, urine, and shit underneath the pig's feet. The rank ammonia-filled air is typical and doesn't faze the pig farmers. They live with the stench daily, and their nasal passages are numbed from years of exposure.

Unlike the pungent aspects, there is one thing neither of the men has grown accustomed to: the amount of strenuous work. Having no one else besides them to assist on the farm, they are fatigued, and sweat seeps through their work overalls with every shovel of shit and each scoop of feed. They have reached the point of the taxing day when they no longer care how much dirt and perspiration stains their skin; their thoughts are only on completing the day's chores so that they can retire to the house for dinner and bed.

Although the moment cannot come fast enough, Tom's heavy boots drag beneath him, slowing him down. He wants a break but knows it's a luxury he won't get. To stay on his grandparents' good side, he must do twice the work to prove his worth and maintain a roof over his head. The idea that one day he may inherit the farm is the only thing that keeps him going and is the key to preserving his sanity, which has proven to be a bit more difficult for him recently.

His challenging upbringing fuels the internal struggles he has neglected to address, and increasingly, he feels the heaviness of his mental anguish worsening. As it chips away at his psychological and physical health, the chaos has induced restless nights and substantial weight loss. Even though his stark shift of appearance acts as a cry for help, his grandparents overlook it as a concern, tokening it solely to a growth spurt.

Tom finds little joy in his existence, and his impending eighteenth birthday seems increasingly less thrilling of an idea. Instead, the concept terrifies him because, unlike earlier in his life, when he could seamlessly shut off his anger, the combination of his physical exhaustion and his recent bouts of insomnia has made holding back his pent-up rage more challenging. Each day, his fear grows that the lurking darkness will surface.

The only hope he has left to manage his fluctuating sanity is provided by knowing that his career path has some certainty. However, to maintain his profession in farming and ultimately be rewarded with the family business, he must keep his composure around his grandparents to retain their trust. Tom is confident he can convince them he is nothing like his drug-addicted mother or deadbeat father by proving himself through his hard work and exhibiting a well-thought-out facade that masks his underlying personality quirks, especially his easily triggered anger and disturbing fascinations.

As Tom's legs give out from being on his feet since sunrise, the aroma of cooking pork cuts through the tangy scent of manure, and the smell of supper provides hope that the arduous day has ended. Typically, when the smell of roasting meat from the kitchen's oven wafts across the field to the barn, it is their cue to wrap up their work and head inside for the day. However, looking at his grandfather, Tom notices something is different; he is ignoring the usual schedule.

Regardless, he brushes off the odd behavior. Acting like nothing is wrong, he straightens the stray hay bales against the wall and checks the pigs' feed as part of his usual routine of wrapping up for the day. Upon completing the task, he sees that only a few pellets remain at the bottom of the fifty-gallon metal can. If they ration the feed between the hogs, it will last the growing herd a day at best.

The sight causes his fingers to fidget nervously, and he quickly becomes concerned that his complacency is to blame. Without shifting his gaze, he shouts to his grandfather in an attempt to cover the possible oversight, "Want me to put a feed order in for pick up tomorrow?"

Before he can finish the question, his grandfather shakes his head. "No, son, that won't be necessary." Something is on his mind, and it becomes apparent when his eyes divert from Tom to the pitchforks hanging on the barn wall. Redirecting the conversation from the feed topic, he reaches over to lift two from their hangers, then shamelessly continues. "I think it's time we talk."

The sudden shift in the seriousness of his demeanor confirms Tom's deepest fear that something is up, and he puts the lid back on the feed can, giving his grandfather his full attention. Noticing that he is struggling to remove the farm tools from their mounted positions, he instantly walks over to help, but by the time he gets there, his grandfather has already retrieved both pitchforks and stands, holding one in each hand. Then, without saying a word, he extends one in Tom's direction.

Fighting exhaustion, Tom reluctantly reaches out and takes the tool from his grasp, and they enter the pen with the pigs.

Tom's grandfather avoids eye contact with his grandson as he runs the metal combs through the dirt. Then, while scooping up a heap of straw bedding to shake out, he clears his throat to break the room's tension. "The farm is not doing well," he says. His somber tone exudes his feelings of disappointment.

Tom hides his emotionless expression by pretending to work.

His grandfather focuses on poking a pile of dirt near his feet to ease his guilt. Wanting to get the conversation over swiftly, he quickens the pace of his speech. "It's been no secret we are hurting for cash. You've seen how much food we have left for the herd to eat with your own two eyes. Since the hog broker started paying us less for the livestock going to slaughter, the farm's profitability hasn't been the same. It's as if he wants to run us out of business, and we must face that it's becoming harder to take care of the animals, let alone to make a living compared to past years.

As sad as it may be, we have to move forward," he says as he avoids eye contact. "So, with that being said, your grandmother and I have been talking, and we feel that with you turning eighteen tomorrow, you should begin thinking about flying the coop."

Blindsided by the conversation's unexpected shift in direction, Tom stops sifting through the dirt, and his demeanor becomes tense. With a passive chuckle, he tries to make a joke about the discussion to lighten the mood. "What are you trying to say? That I need to get the hell out?" he asks.

Even though his grandfather knows the brash rephrasing precisely restates what he'd meant, hearing it repeated aloud makes him uncomfortable. Knowing there is no going back, he seizes the moment to get the rest of his thoughts off his chest. He stammers, "Well, your grandmother thought we should discuss it over dinner, but I thought a manly heart-to-heart would be best."

Picturing his grandmother involved in plotting his exile from the farm strikes a nerve deep in Tom's core, and his jaw clenches as he processes the information.

His grandfather instantly recognizes the barn's tension and sees that Tom is no longer contributing to the conversation. His words nervously stumble in circles as he attempts to make him understand. Trying a different approach, he throws a few of their hardships in his face to trigger empathy regarding their decision. "The last thing I want to do is stress the poor woman out. She already has enough heaviness on her heart over your momma and all," he says.

Referring to the woman who abandoned him at age five as his "momma" strikes a nerve in Tom, and the inference does not incite the response his grandfather hoped for. Tom's heartbeat accelerates, and the blood boils in his veins. It's as if he is again disregarded, watching the only life he knew disappear through the social worker's rear window.

Having nowhere in the barn to take refuge from the one-on-one, he tries to stomach his spiraling emotions and repress his true feelings regarding the conversation. In a quick attempt to stop the escalation of his rage, he tries to maintain his composure by focusing his attention on any work in front of him that he can do. Tom pushes around the dirt with the pitchfork to no avail, and his anger worsens. He can no longer restrain his disagreement.

In an irrational outburst, he breaks his silence and disgorges his bottled emotions. "But...but... I don't understand. I work my ass off day in and day out to help around this place," he says; his teeth clench to keep his mouth from spewing something else he may regret.

Irritated by the boy's show of selfishness, the older man believes his grandson is overreacting to the news and responds to his dismay with a simple shrug.

Even though his point has come across loud and clear, he finds it necessary to add to the topic in hopes it will incite a verbal confirmation that he understands how and why they came to their decision. "Wait until you are our age; maybe you will look back on this moment and better understand the situation. We are both getting older and want to retire. With you in the picture, that's not possible. You should be thankful that we took you in for the past several years. Remember, you are your parent's responsibility, not ours," he says.

Tom lowers his eyes away from his grandfather to escape the verbal torment, and his inability to remain in control causes his fists to grip the round wooden handle tighter.

The older man attempts to make eye contact with his grandson, but the young man's eyes remain fixed on the ground. Tom's submissive nature makes his grandfather believe his words are finally getting through. Chuckling with relief, he continues, "We didn't plan on assuming the financial burden of supporting another child past the one we already had." He smiles to put a positive spin on things. "Now, we don't expect you to go today; you can stay a week after your birthday to give you time to pack your things and find a job."

As the older man's voice rambles on, Tom scans his withered frame, thinking the familiarity of his appearance will evoke a sense of understanding toward the decision, but rather than a representation of family, the shell of a stranger greets his eye. He sees the figure as a monster, kicking him out into the cold.

His debilitating anxiety fills his ears with a deafening ring, and everything around him quiets. With each movement of his mouth, his words exit his lips as mumbling garble, adding to his swirling mind, and he is unable to track any of the content of the conversation past the news that he must move out of the only place he calls home. Feeling deceived, he blankly stares at the male figure he once considered an example of how a man should act.

The betrayal takes him back to a vivid memory from his childhood—when he watched four police officers drag his violent father out of the old farmhouse and haul him off to jail. Tom never saw his face again; it was only a year or two before he confronted the wrong inmate with a homemade knife and wound up dead. Staring at the man before him, he views them as the same; they're both liars who don't value family.

Abruptly, he hears the ringing in his ears soften, and his grandfather's waving hands catch his attention. "Tom, you hear me?" he asks. Still stunned by the news and unable to knock the comparison from his mind, he nods silently.

Thinking Tom is taking it well, the older man finds the lack of combativeness a telling indication of his grandson's mature understanding of the situation. His face softens with a smile to impart a bonding moment as he shares some positive news to turn the mood around. "What do you say we go in and eat some supper? I feel like that's enough work for the day," he says as he turns to face the pen's exit.

Tom finds the man's carefree demeanor condescending, and he glares at his turned back, replying to his comments only with a sneer. The movement of his grandfather languidly walking away causes his eyes to squint with anger, and every emotion trapped in his being boils in his core.

The horrible thought of leaving the pigs repeats in his brain, and concern over their futures sours the lining of his gut.

With the pitchfork still in hand, his obsessive stare remains fixated on the sweat accumulating on the older man's hunched back. His perception of the situation shifts, now viewing the man's withdrawal as one of cowardice. He is sure that his hasty retreat, like an aged antelope running to escape a ravenous lion, is solely due to the fear of his supremacy.

His thoughts spiral and his vision turns black. The pigs feed off his unstable energy and shift theirs to match the chaos consuming his mind.

Amid the disconcerted air, small timid oinks sound near Tom's feet, and he feels something softly nudging his knee. Shifting his focus to look, he sees his favorite piglet nestling against him; her name is Olive. Her tiny black snout, which has earned her the nickname, wiggles with each snort. Along with her unique nose, her body's coloring differs from the others. She has distinct markings of bright brown spots on her pink skin, and her stature is substantially smaller than the rest of the herd. In the crowded group of hogs, she sticks out as the runt of the bunch—or, as Tom calls her, the outsider. To him, she is a loner, just like him, and they understand one another. Olive is the friend he had not found in his like kind but always wanted.

As her tiny damp nose rubs up against his pant leg, he thinks of how they may hurt her when he leaves, and the horrific thought causes his grip to tighten around the wooden handle. Tom knows firsthand the terror of abandonment and can't fathom the idea of her tiny squealing cries pleading for help and him not being there to save her. She would lose faith in him; he could not live with himself if that happened.

The excruciating idea fuels a rush of adrenaline through his pounding heart, body, and limbs, causing his hands to tremble. The emotions he has worked so hard to suppress explode to the surface, and his opinion shoots from his throat like an erupting volcano. "No!" he screams as his head convulsively shakes from side to side. Imagining again being torn from everything he loves causes his vision to distort with blurring colors of black and red. "You can't do this to me!" As an unbearable heat runs through his veins, rage possesses his bones. Tom's facade is lowered for the first time, and his true self is exposed.

The abruptness of the defiant words stops his grandfather in his tracks, and deep down, he knows the earlier encounter had been easier than expected. Even though he is not shocked by the sudden turn in behavior, he wishes Tom would accept their choices and move on with his life. Irritated, he attempts to muster up the patience to rehash each reason for their decision. He releases a loud sigh as he prepares to face his grandson to reiterate the key points of their prior conversation.

The sight of his grandfather's pivoting body evokes an instinctual survival response to surge from the deepest part of the boy's gut. At that moment, there is nothing to lose and everything to gain. He knows if he cannot force him to change his mind, his life will be damned forever. Darkness fills his entire being, to the point of exuding an icy blackness through his corneas.

As his grandfather makes eye contact with Tom, it becomes clear something isn't right; he observes no sign of humanity hidden behind his glossed-over pupils. Instead, they exude a pitiless indifference toward those who do not obey their demands. He had seen this once before—the same emotionless glare Tom's father displayed immediately following the discovery of him standing over the body of his dead daughter, Tom's mother. The callous look made it clear that her death wasn't an accidental overdose, as documented by the county coroner. Regardless of his not-guilty plea, the man's history of violence solidified his belief that he was to blame. Tom and his father's callous stare bordered on sociopathy and made it evident that neither held any regard for anyone's life but their own.

Never having recognized that side of Tom before, he is terrified by the connection. The realization causes his pupils to dilate with fear. He holds his free hand in front of him as a sign of surrender and fumbles to find the right words to trigger the teen's re-engagement. "Maybe I misspoke. Let's have dinner, and we can discuss this misunderstanding." In a panic, he makes no sudden movements but calmy begins to back away toward the gate of the pen.

Tom smirks at his grandfather's sudden change of heart, seeing straight through his attempt to escape inconspicuously. Feeding off his angst, Tom releases an animalistic grunt, and his feet push off the dirt floor as he charges toward his grandfather with his pitchfork extended in front of him like a jousting lance.

The older man's eyes widen with fear as the implement's piercing tines drive deeply into his stomach's soft wall, filling the tin-walled barn with the ungodly sounds of rupturing cartilage and bone. Everything plays in slow motion as the sharp edge of the prongs spears through his torso and exits his back.

Having never spoken his truth before, Tom feels empowered for the first time in his life. Allowing his rage to guide his actions, he keeps eye contact with the older man while driving the pitchfork deeper. After an added twist of the handle, the sloshing of his loose organs hitting the dirt floor brings him a sense of happiness he has never felt before.

The older man's pain response is delayed due to his state of shock. Blood fills his lungs and drips from his mouth, his fingers loosen around the wooden handle of the pitchfork in his hand, and it falls to the ground. His feet stumble backward, and his legs collapse beneath him.

The sound of the man's body hitting the ground snaps Tom's mind back to reality, and the gruesome sight causes his hands to shake uncontrollably. However, it isn't remorse that fuels his anxiety, but rather the fear of possibly being unable to spin the situation to paint his innocence that provokes his disquiet.

Wanting to punish and calm himself simultaneously, he slaps the side of his head with his hands. "Why... why did he have to say that? Oh, God, what did you do, Tom? What did you do?" he asks. As his feet pace the pen, he continues his spiral. "They are going to lock you up, just like your father. You proved them right. You are just like him."

His grandfather lies helplessly in the dirt. His body spasms and the irreversible mutilation causes his lungs to hack up blood. Through his last moment's delirium, his shaking fingers feel for the rusty implement protruding from his core; then, his hands fall beside him as he takes a final gasping breath.

The noise strikes a nerve in Tom, and, unable to think clearly, he runs his finger through his hair while pacing the pen. The pigs scream with wild excitement over the smell of a fresh kill.

Every sound overwhelms him, exacerbating the deterioration of his mental state. In a desperate attempt to redirect his negative thoughts, he laughs maniacally. "What am I going to do? I can't go to jail. I'm not my dad. Come on, think. We both know you are not stupid," he says.

Still flustered by the turn of events, he buries his face in his hands and, mid-thought, hears an unfamiliar sound. He lifts his head to look in the commotion's direction and observes the pigs swarming the corpse. Worried their interference may make matters worse, he rushes over to the herd, neurotically waving his hands to shoo them away, but a peculiar development stops him dead in his tracks.

The sounds of crunching bones echo between the tin walls of the barn as they swiftly devour half of his grandfather's body. The taste of the flesh fuels a profound pleasure in them he has never witnessed before, and unlike their typical snorts, their snouts exude shrills of gratitude.

Their enjoyment causes his eyes to brighten with an idea, and, not wanting to interfere with their happiness, he takes a step back to allow them to enjoy their meal peacefully. He chuckles with relief. "I should have known they wouldn't let me down. They never do," he says.

Smiling from ear to ear, he revels in each penalizing sound of bones grinding between their teeth, and the clamor resonates freedom. He notices them nearing the end of their feast and carefully approaches, warmly reaching out his hand to pet each of their backs in a show of gratitude. "Good little piggies. You were hungry. I am glad you enjoyed your supper." Their loud snorts in response to his praise make his smile widen.

They snuffle around the dirt, taking one final sweep for the remains. Finding nothing left to eat, they disperse about the pen and return to their usual way of life.

As they mill around in a typical fashion, Tom scans the former site of their congregated indulgence and notices they overlooked something. A small skewered piece of bowel is still on the pitchfork's blood-soaked end.

Even though he finds its sausage-like consistency disgusting, he wants to be a part of the family festivities. As his hand snatches the tool's handle, his lips loudly whistle, calling the pigs to return, and they come running in a frenzy.

Scraping the forked end against the dirt, he nudges the piece of organ off the sharp tines and then stabs the pointy end into the ground, leaving it in wait for later. The animals snort chaotically as they fight over the last piece of flesh.

He glances around the metal structure's interior, notices an unfamiliar crack in the tin of the barn wall, and begins fixating on how it has gotten there. At the peak of his curiosity, he views the dark sky through the breach and suddenly realizes how much time has elapsed. He heads toward the gate, grabbing his grandfather's clean pitchfork from the ground as he passes.

Upon exiting the pen, he ensures the entrance is latched, hangs the pitchfork in its designated hook on the wall, then takes one last look back at the pigs. "Don't worry. Nothing will separate us," he says in a whisper. The pigs oink in reply.

As he shuts the large sliding door behind him, he realizes he has forgotten to turn the barn light off. Certain the pigs would prefer not to be left in darkness, he chooses to leave it on.

A cool breeze brushes against his cheek and causes his lungs to release a long sigh. As the wind rustles the leaves, it carries the sound of a woman's whisper to his ears, and, recognizing the voice as his grandmother, he turns to look.

Nothing is there.

Glaring in the house's direction, he sees her outline in the front window, setting the kitchen table, and he knows what he must do. "One to go," he says with a smirk.

Calculatingly, with a purpose-filled walk, he counts each heavy step toward the house's front door. Then, taking a moment, he pauses at the base of the porch's stairs, admiring what will soon be his before he enters.

Chapter Three

DO YOU LIKE PIGS?

After, Bellmore, Ohio

Upon sunrise, daily routines returned to normal, but nothing was the same. The previous night, a monster restrained for the better of eighteen years was permanently unleashed.

Deep cleaning, some repairs, and his grandfather's moonshine stores have helped him remain mentally unscathed from his actions.

Reveling in the recompense left to him as the only remaining kin of the elderly couple has squelched any sense of guilt. Upon attaining his wish-fulfillment of inheriting the farm, he's returned to his usual reticent demeanor, containing any emotions he believes would trigger the darkness to react viciously.

Knowing what he is capable of, he decides it's best to remove himself from human interaction by living a life of isolation. Over time, he comes to love being alone and the predictability of his daily schedule.

As for any residual mourning over his grandparents' deaths, it never occurs to him that being unfazed over their extermination should be cause for concern. Honestly, he's relieved not to have to see their faces or fight over the coffee pot with them each morning.

He sustains himself by living off the farm's extensive pantry of home-canned goods, gardening, and scavenging for his grandparents' secret stashes of rainy-day and retirement funds. With each discovered hoard, he provides a stable but conservative food supply for the pigs. This is the only time he finds some validity in his grandfather's final words—fewer people living in the home indeed assures financial sustainability.

As we reflect on his vow of isolation, you may be curious how he can live alone without raising suspicion and still attain grain for the herd without making trips to the feed store. To avoid face-to-face interactions, he uses the home's landline to call the local farm store to arrange noncontact monthly grain deliveries.

Once a month, he places an envelope with cash in the mailbox at the end of the dirt drive. In exchange, the feed store leaves bags of pellets for the pigs. Then, on delivery day, after the trade occurs, and when he can no longer hear the engine of the field truck, he drives the farm's old ford tractor and trailer to retrieve it.

Over time, his quiet demeanor has made him likable to the members of the small town; in fact, no one has ever had a bad word to say about him because he's remained unseen for the most part. As a result, they rarely have any opportunities to converse with Tom, and their naivety proves beneficial.

Unbeknownst to him, no one gives his solitude a second thought due to the grandfather's constant talk about retiring to Florida. In fact, everyone but Tom knew that they did not intend to spend their remaining years on the farm.

His grandfather had reveled in the kudos given by others when he told them that even though it would be a financial strain, he only felt it right to pass the farm to Tom after his dreadful childhood. Of course, it had never been his intent, but he loved the attention over spewing his empty generosities.

Not privy to the town chatter, Tom was confident his brilliance was the reason for their lack of suspicion over the grandparents' sudden disappearance, not that the entire town of seventy-five assumed that the two had permanently gone south for warmer weather.

Everyone agreed to anything he requested, giving their answers without hesitation—it was the least they could do for a local boy who had faced such childhood difficulties.

Having nothing and no one to alter his daily predictability makes his moods more manageable. For once, he finds his violent thoughts subdued and is quite content with his position in life. He believes he is a changed man.

Year after year, he successfully locks himself away on the remote property that makes up the farm. Living his purpose of taking care of the pigs, he upholds his vow never to sell the animals for meat, and, feeling indebted to them for his freedom, he lives each day to honor their existence and mourn their natural deaths.

For nearly five years, his plan appears foolproof. That is, until one summer's day when he finds he has exhausted the last of his money on feed.

Trying to bide time, he shares his remaining jars of peaches with the animals while thinking of a plan to find an alternative source of income. Though he still wants to restrict his human interactions, he knows he has limited options for generating revenue without leaving the farm.

He heads into the house, scanning the home for things he can sell for cash. He catches sight of his grandfather's *Popular Mechanics* car-repair guide sitting on a shelf in the living room, and an idea comes to mind. The older man had believed in doing everything himself and had collected miscellaneous tools over the years that he kept in an old wooden tool chest in the barn. Tom has used them a few times to repair this and that around the farm after their passing.

Being most comfortable talking with the grain shop owner after several years of placing orders over the phone, he calls and asks that he spread the word about his newly formed mechanic shop. Not wanting to deal with additional phone calls, he makes a deal with the store owner that if he does the scheduling, he can keep a percentage of the sales for his efforts. Of course, the man complies.

With *Popular Mechanics* as his guide, Tom drums up sufficient business to allow him and his herd adequate money to survive. As long as everyone has food, it's enough for him to remain happy.

Lacking consistent human interaction, the pigs become his only form of companionship, and he crafts a mattress of straw to sleep in their pen. As a result, he becomes severely codependent on the herd, and they develop a mutual understanding of one another's devotion.

Their presence alone makes him feel content.

As each day passes, he finds it more difficult to separate himself from the comfort of his four-legged family, and he sleeps in the barn more nights than not. Eventually, he only enters the main house when necessary.

The more settled he becomes with sharing a lifestyle with the animals, the more he shifts those necessities to the barn. If he's hungry, he grabs a handful of grain from the bin and regularly uses the dirt floor of the pigpen as his bathroom. For the most part, aside from the fact that Tom must generate revenue to sustain their existence, both Tom and the herd live identically.

Typically, there's an unspoken rule when he works on customers' vehicles. Preferring to work in silence, he does not entertain conversations with the clients.

But, just like everything else in his life, that eventually changes.

It's mid-June, and as the sun aggressively beats down from above, beads of sweat form on the apples of his cheeks. Patiently sitting in front of the tin barn on an upside-down five-gallon bucket, his hand carefully wipes away the droplets of sweat. His lungs inhale a deep breath to calm himself as his fingers migrate to his forehead to shield his eyes from the glare.

Trying to get a better look down the dirt driveway, he fixates his gaze on the red flag of the rust-tarnished silver mailbox to pass the time.

The feed store has scheduled another car for him to work on. He never asks for details regarding the owner's identity, preferring only to know the vehicle basics, such as the make and model, so that he can identify the car upon its arrival. Remaining detached allows him to avoid small talk with clients and eliminates the possibility of them overstaying their welcome or asking personal questions. All he cares about is the money, and he has no interest in changing his antisocial behavior.

Tom hears the sound of a rough-running engine before he spots the red Chevy convertible approaching in the distance. As it gets closer, it is clear that the body has imperfections, and its dirt-smudged cream canvas top is held together by silver duct tape.

He immediately recognizes that the car meets the description and stands to his feet. As it rolls down the driveway toward him, dirt kicks into the air, and its engine's rattling knocks become louder.

He finds the client's later-than-expected arrival irritating and the clunking racket agitating to his ears. He winces over his displeasure.

Tom cannot see the driver through the swirling dust, so he blindly waves his hands to flag them to park by the barn. With a screech of the brakes, its balding tires stop.

His pupils scan the unkempt nature of the car through the churning dirt cloud. Then, as he tries to make out the driver through the windshield, he hears the driver-side handle click, and the door swings open.

It is a young woman with strawberry blond pin-curls secured half-up with a banana clip. Her long, curly bangs wildly cascade down the sides of her round face, past her rhinestone cat-eye-shaped tortoiseshell sunglasses, to her cheekbones. She wears a light pink gingham button-up sleeveless top tied at her navel, and a tight-fitting pair of dark-wash capris cuffed mid-calve. Her short red-polished nails match her lipstick and the color of her car. Following the color trend are the red shoes on her feet and the purse tucked under her arm.

As she steps out of the vehicle, her pupils, hidden by the dark lenses, brazenly scan the property until eventually landing on Tom's squinting eyes. Concerned she hasn't made enough of an entrance; she slams the driver's door shut behind her. "Sorry I'm late, sugar," she says as she takes off her sunglasses while approaching him. "You would not believe my morning."

Unlike Tom's usual clientele, this one is a woman, and her presence leaves him speechless. The last woman he exchanged a complete sentence with was his grandmother, so he finds her flouncy company foreign. As his throat becomes dry, he nervously gulps and nods.

Getting closer, she folds her glasses and hangs the sparkly frames from the front of her partially unbuttoned blouse. She finds Tom's lanky stature and gruff appearance attractive. Used to being surrounded by the town's lowlifes, he smells like a hard-working man to her rather than thinking he reeks of musk. She flirtatiously pushes her cleavage together. "They didn't tell me I was going to meet a tall looker like you," she says with a smirk.

Her chattiness flusters him, and his cheeks blush a rosy hue as he glances down at the dirt. Something about her appears familiar, but he can't place his recollection. Before he can think of a response, she bounces closer, and a strong waft of floral-scented perfume flows through the air and into his nostrils. The combination of the residual hovering dust from her arrival and the pungent smell causes him to sneeze uncontrollably.

Unaccustomed to a man not fawning over her, she brushes off the unusual indifference and purses her lips. "You've got some nice pigs over there. I saw them as I pulled in," she says.

He glances over his shoulder at the closed barn door and scratches his head. "Thanks. They are my family," he says.

After finally receiving a response, she asserts herself more and giggles. "Isn't that just the most precious thing I ever did hear?" she says as she gallops in the barn's direction. "I love animals. Why don't you introduce us?"

His ignorance over how to handle her abrasive personality paralyzes him with fear, and his only defense is to timidly lift his finger to urge her to stop. She pays no attention to his communication issues and opens the stiff sliding door with a massive heave.

As he timidly watches her make her way inside, he nervously twiddles his dirty fingertips. Even though she has no knowledge of the dark events that have occurred within the tin walls, his mind circulates every what-if scenario. *If she says anything or lets on to what I did, I'll get rid of her like the others.*

Noticing he is not following her like a lost puppy, she pokes her head through the doorframe to look at him. "You coming? You can't honestly expect me to give myself a tour," she says.

Her voice snaps him out of his daydream, and his craving to kill, resurfacing, makes him smirk. With a jolt, he moves forward to follow her inside.

She takes his enthusiasm as a sign of flirtation and smiles as she lets him lead the way to the pen. As they approach, the pigs happily oink to say hello. Her eyes light up. "Wow, they are the most gorgeous creatures I have ever seen," she says.

For the first time in his life, he believes he witnesses the same spark in someone else's eyes that he exhibits when looking at the pigs. He can't help but stare at her side profile.

She leans over the railing to pet the animals. Olive emerges from the herd and approaches her hand. Wanting to be scratched, the now-grown sow nudges her wet black nose against her palm.

As he watches the interaction, the familiarity of her appearance comes to him. He is in disbelief. She looks identical to his favorite pig, Olive.

He watches their noses turn up in unison and scrunch when they make a noise or smile. Their round-shaped faces have matching small narrow-set eyes that are the same color of brownish blue, and both lips have a similar thin shape. His eyes widen at the revelation.

Sensing him staring at her back stops her hand mid-scratch, and her break in attention causes the pigs to let out loud oinks of disappointment. She straightens her posture to turn and look at him. "Everything okay?" she asks.

His eyes drift to a dirt smudge left by the railing across her chest, and he nods with a smile. "Yes. Why do you ask?" he says. Her hands brush off her shirt as her eyes scan the pen of pigs. "Oh, no reason," she says.

Something peculiar catches her attention. It's a straw mattress lying on the dirt floor in the corner of the pen. "What's that?" Her finger points in reference to the object. He slowly walks up behind her and places his hand on the railing. Embarrassed, he murmurs his answer under his breath. "I sometimes like to sleep in here," he says.

Even though she thinks his response is odd, she covers her confusion with a fake smile and clears her throat. "That must mean you are lonely," she says as she steps closer to him. He shrugs as he stares with a smile at the cluster of pigs.

Having dated cheaters and men with drug addictions in the past, she can accept the minor quirk if that is the worst thing about him.

To engage him in conversation, she redirects the topic to learn more about his passion. "So do you sell them, or what?" she asks. Before she can finish the question, hearing someone mention selling them causes him to cut her off with a burst of anger. "God, no. They are my family; I keep them all. You don't sell family," he says.

His agitated behavior signals her to switch her emotions to sympathy. " Oh, of course, absolutely not," she says. She briefly pauses to formulate her strategy before continuing. "Why would you, anyway? You are a car-repair business owner." Her eyes look back to the pigs, and her voice gathers excitement. "Say, have you ever shown them at the local fair?"

As his anger dissipates, he looks at his snorting family. "Uh-uh," he says as he shakes his head. "We are comfortable here, so that's where we stay."

She lifts her hand to nudge his shoulder play-fully. "With pigs as beautiful as yours, why would you not enter them? You know there's prize money involved, right?" Without hesitation, he turns to look at her. The thought intrigues him. "Oh? How much?" he asks.

"I suppose it's only a few hundred bucks or so, but it all adds up," she says with a smirk.

His mind becomes filled with a vision of others applauding his pigs' beauty, and he smiles. "When is it?" he asks.

She focuses on him with affectionate eyes. "July," she replies.

At first, the idea of the extra cash freeing him from having to work on strangers' vehicles excites him, but then he remembers that his farm truck is broken down, leaving him no way to transport the animals to the fair. "Maybe next year, after I have time to fix the truck we use to haul them," he says with a sigh.

Noticing his expression of defeat, she glances at his hand resting on the railing and gently places hers on top of his. "I believe in those pigs and think they need a chance to shine like the stars that they are. I'll drive you there in my convertible if you want," she says confidently.

Her willingness to help him sparks a fluttering in his stomach that he has never felt before. She seems so understanding of his qualities that he had been sure would be deemed peculiar. Before thinking over his answer, he belts, "We would love that."

She hops up and down with excitement while clapping her hands together, pausing only to gently brush the bouncing curls from her face. As Tom watches her, he visualizes his favorite pig in her place, displaying the same mannerisms which make him comfortable. His face turns bashful, and he nods in the car's direction. "Well, if you're gonna hold up your end of the bargain, I suppose we'd better fix that car of yours," he says.

She grins at him as she places her sunglasses on the short bridge of her nose. "I suppose you are right," she says.

Before he knows what is happening, she takes hold of his arm. Her fingers lightly grasp his skin, mimicking the touch of a tiny pig's hoof, and his heart flutters.

Together, they make their way outside. He closes the barn behind them and bolts to the car. As he opens the hood, he notices a loose spark plug and tightens it. "That should do the trick," he says.

As she walks behind him to observe his repair, she holds back a secret: she knows how to fix cars. Being an only child of a father who was a mechanic, she was given no option but to become proficient in auto repair.

On a hunt to find a husband and having no luck in love with the men in the small town, she heard people talk about the lonely bachelor living in seclusion and thought it was worth a shot to meet him. So, to do that, she staged a minor car problem that she knew wouldn't be detrimental to her drive to his place.

With a smirk, she pats his back. "It is sure nice to be in the presence of a man who knows how to fix a car. I'm just so clueless about that kind of thing," she says.

As he shuts the hood, he chuckles. "It's nothing, ma'am," he says, looking at his feet.

She tries to make eye contact with him. "'Ma'am' is what they call my mother. My name is Claudia, or Claud for short," she says as she sticks out her hand.

His eyeline raises to meet hers, and he lightly grips her hand to shake. "I'm Tom," he says.

She continues to latch on, thriving in their moment of reciprocal human touch. "So, what do I owe you for your fine work?" she asks, flirtatiously biting her lip.

Tom becomes caught up in the idea of his pigs becoming famous and wants to be alone with his thoughts. He begins his retreat by retracting his hands to his sides. "For you, just that ride to the fair next month," he says.

Excited about her new possibilities, she rushes to the driver's side with a pep in her step and, turning back, gives him a flirtatious smile. "You got it, handsome," she says. "I will see you July 12 at 9 a.m. sharp."

She gives him one last glance to test the waters of their connection. He reciprocates with a smile and cuts the conversation short by signaling his agreement with a quick thumbs up.

Eager to preserve the moment, she swiftly reaches for the door handle and hops into the driver's seat. She turns the key, the engine purrs, and she fights back a chuckle as she smiles from ear to ear, showing her excitement over its improved performance. Then, revving the car's engine, she backs up and speeds out of the driveway.

Tom's eyes follow the exhaust trail until he can no longer see it in the distance. Then, unable to hold back his excitement, he sprints to the barn and flings the door open. "Did you hear that, everyone?" he shouts.

He dashes to the pen's gate, lets himself inside, and sits on the ground. "She's going to make you famous. We may never have to work again."

The pigs rub against his sides as they swarm him to fight for attention.

As he gives his rounds of pats, he analyzes each pig to choose the one to represent the herd, and his eyes lock on Olive. "I know it's no secret, but with your beauty, you're the best bet to win," he says.

She snorts in response and clacks her teeth together. Tom lightly kisses her nose. "You are perfect. Do you know that? Maybe we should get married," he says with a chuckle.

The pig gets closer to nuzzle her snout into the crease of his neck. He feels her warmth through her soft damp nose. "Let's agree, right here and now, that if you win, we will marry. You are the only one I need," he says in an oddly sincere tone.

The entire herd squeals with excitement as he hugs Olive. Reveling in their unified grunts, he chuckles. "Looks like we have their blessing," he says with a grin.

Nothing had ever been more perfect to him. He was finally living the dream he had always wanted.

Chapter Four

HERE TO WIN

Everyone has heard the saying *Time flies when you're having fun*, and Tom, like many, has no immunity to that cliché. He becomes hyper-focused on the upcoming event of the small-town fair's pig jamboree—the days leading up to the event pass quicker than he and his carnivorous family would expect.

The pressure of prepping for the competition takes over his life; before he knows it, there's no time left for anything else in the day. To him, the choice is simple. Personal sacrifices must be made to be a winner, and his already-minimalist approach to self-care is the first on the docket to suffer.

His obsessive fixation on pampering the bristly creatures sucks every ounce of his individuality dry, like a leech's fervent draining of a victim.

Fanaticism wreaks havoc on his life, and losing structure annihilates his self-esteem.

One night, when he's fast asleep on his straw mattress, he has one remarkably lucid dream where the pigs convey that there is no other option but to regain control. Even though they've guided him to alter his routine, he takes full credit for the shift, proclaiming daily to the herd that he alone has determined an alteration in his behavior was the right thing to do.

Everything seems suitable for dear Tom, and his reformation from chaos appears to make him happy on the outside, but some things are hidden from the naked eye and, like a silent disease, brew deep in his gut.

His battle to regain control is not without cost. Unbeknownst to Tom, the radical transition aids in pulling apart each tiny thread that barely holds together his fragile patchwork peace of mind.

The redundancy of the new routine initially causes his personality to be a bit more temperamental, but as his life settles into a seemingly happy compromise, his patience improves.

Within his new pattern of living, his schedule is as follows: he bathes Olive both morning and evening, hoping to produce a perfect coat; then, in between grooming sessions, he fits in hours of practicing showmanship, using his grandfather's old walking cane to drive her around the pen. They repeat the schedule daily—eat, sleep, groom, train, groom. All their day-to-day activities are simple yet effective, and he is enthusiastic about his hands shaping a herd of champions.

Tom's unlimited time with the pigs exacerbates his obsession with winning, which becomes the only thing on his mind. He sleeps next to them on his makeshift mattress so that when he wakes each morning bright and early, he can promptly start his schedule before the summer heat fills the barn.

The steadfast routine raises his confidence and keeps his beating heart's tempo consistently calm.

Until an interruption occurs.

It's a week before the competition, to be exact. As the sun hoists itself over the flat terrain, each cloud, shaped like a cotton ball, takes its place, scattering across the dark sky.

Usually, he favors taking a moment to watch the earth wake up and revels in knowing he's beaten the world to the punch of starting a productive day. But this particular morning, he finds the beauty of the sunrise degraded by its twenty-minute-early arrival and the stagnant air's humidity.

The schedule's non-predictable nature innately causes a peculiar knot to form in the pit of his stomach. Because his obsessive-compulsive tendencies already make him prone to being overly observant of minor details, there is no need to check the time to know something is off or to consult with his companions regarding the inconsistency. Instead, he tries to control his disquiet by subconsciously pushing the information into the back of his brain.

Wanting to return to the normalcy of his routine, he quickly gives Olive her morning bath and, once finished, holds her damp body tightly in his arms to calm his emotional unease. As he sits on the packed dirt floor, cuddling the sow inside the pen, he observes rays of sunlight peeking through the break in the barn's tin siding that, due to further deterioration, is filleted back like a peeled banana. The tampered-with tin perfectly frames the splash of warm colors that highlight the sky like a spilled bottle of bright orange paint.

As the overflow of illumination continues to creep through the opening, it projects upon Tom's cheek, caressing his skin. He briefly closes his eyes to enjoy the warming sensation fully.

The beautiful sight causes his arms to squeeze tighter around the animal's stiff body. He scoots their entwined position closer to the breach to watch the rest of the daybreak. His lungs inhale the air, and the pig's distinct aroma soothes him.

Olive trembles from the recent bath, and he leans to the side to share the light's heat with her chilled body. His eyes fixate on her bristles as they dry, and each of his spindly fingers takes a lengthy turn combing through her long coat. As the spiky hair runs between his fingertips, his smile showcases his devotion, and refraining from speaking; he listens to the pattern of her soft oinks. Overwhelmed by her perfection in the lighting, his upper body leans slightly forward, and he kisses the tip of her snout.

Olive echoes Tom's happiness, with slight purring sounds from her wiggling nose and her lips curling up to mimic a smile. Her eyes lift to peer toward the sun's rays of light warming her skin, then to the caring man holding her.

Tom understands by her gaze that she senses she is special, and he revels in the fact that she doesn't have to utter a single word to confirm it. Together, they share a moment of silence, and even without a word exchanged, it's as though a conversation is taking place.

The overwhelming sensation of emotion creates an itch in the back of Tom's nose, and to relieve himself of the uncomfortable tingle; he releases a long sigh. "If only everyone could be like you, my little button," he says.

A puff of oxygen leaves his nostrils, and the tiny breeze graces the tips of Olive's soft pink ears. The tickling sensation causes them to wiggle.

Tom becomes bashful over her loving expression, and a coy smile forms on his lips. "Who's my sweet little girl?" he asks. The apples of his cheeks turn red as he chuckles flirtatiously. At once, the tip of his pointer finger springs up and lightly taps the center of her snout.

The playful gesture causes Olive to squeal with excitement. Her rib cage shallowly fluctuates with each hyperventilating breath, copying his laughter.

"Though we can understand each other perfectly, I cannot wait until you speak your first words;

it will only be a matter of time. I can only imagine our lengthy conversations with how much we have in common. Our voices will probably be hoarse for months," Tom says through his laughter.

Olive squirms in his arms, and he glances down to look for the reason. Her restlessness causes him to worry that he has offended her. His speech's pace escalates, and his voice's tone goes up an octave. "Don't you worry, little Olive. I will wait as long as it takes for you to find your words. I'm not going anywhere. You are the only one for me.," he says with a snicker.

Her wiggling body calms, and her head nuzzles into the crease of his elbow.

Tom sighs with relief. Carried away with the idea of them jabbering for hours, without thinking, his fingers move down each groove of Olive's spine. Each fingertip shakes uncontrollably as his hand reaches the base of her coiled tail. Like a plague, the tremor moves down the prominent bone of his hand to his wrist. His mind flinches out of his daydream. Trying to contain his weakness, he places his palm on the back of her neck to stabilize it.

Olive turns her head and attempts to nudge his hand with her nose to get him to scratch her back more. But, no matter his mental state, one thing remains consistent: Tom can never say no to his darling sow.

Wanting to please her, he pushes through his lightheaded daze to rub her fur. The softness of her skin underneath his calloused fingertips forms an organic smirk across his lips and grounds him back in his reality. "Your fur sure feels mighty special to the touch," he says.

Olive's coat's soft texture causes him to forget about his troubles and the notion that they could be to blame for his upset stomach. Having set aside the paltry amount he has left of his personal life to cater to the pigs, he has willingly canceled his only income source: the mechanic appointments.

During the weeks leading up to the fair, he's pooled what little savings he has left, including the money allocated for his individual food stipend, and put it toward maintaining the well-being of the animals.

If hunger pains in his gut arise, to compensate for his deprivation, he resorts to grazing on the pig's grain to avoid starving. Even with his sacrifice, he still worries about overeating their sustenance. After chewing the gritty morsels, he spits any hard-to-eat remnants into the trough for the ravenous creatures.

As he continues to pet Olive, the agony worsens in his abdomen, and his stomach growls. Not wanting her to notice his discomfort, he immediately attempts to distract his mind from the lingering hunger pains by darting his eyes toward the barn's tattered siding and admiring the beauty of the sky through the corrugated tin gap.

Mid-stare, his vision blurs, and the lack of control over his body's boisterous demands triggers a deep-rooted frustration. His right hand lifts to the height of his shoulder, and gaining momentum; he moves it to hit his rumbling stomach forcefully. The impact of the harsh blow knocks the wind from his lungs, and as he catches his breath, he captures the sound of another muted growl escaping his gut. "Man up. You only have one week left. Remember, you are doing this for Olive," he says.

Angered by his stomach refusing to quiet down, he fixates on the illuminated clouds, and his mind wanders. In his lucid dream state, he visualizes what it would be like to be engulfed by the warmth of the mustard-colored light rays while snuggling up inside the cotton puffs that unapologetically obstruct the blue sky. The imaginative nature of his happy thoughts levels out his flustered mind, and his shaking hands calm in response.

He takes a deep breath to remind himself why he has made each of his life sacrifices. "They saved you, Tom. Plain and simple. They are your family," he says, as his fixation shifts back to its primary focus, his obsession with winning.

Olive senses his fingers getting close to an itchy spot on her back that she usually cannot reach, and the anticipation causes her shoulder blades to shrug together. Sensing her joy makes him happy, and he returns his eyes to look at her shiny coat of bristles. He takes a moment of peace to revel in the silence encompassing their loving moment.

As he reaches out to rub her ears, he hears an unexpected noise in the distance. His hand lingers in the air as he stops all his movements to listen. Olive releases a few shallow oinks through her snout, and she playfully nibbles at his hand to encourage him to continue his attention.

Tom lifts a finger to his lips and hushes her to quiet. Then, shaping his hand in a funnel, he holds it up to his ear to amplify the advancing noise. He winces upon recognizing the unmistakable rumble of a truck's loud exhaust and the howl of tires kicking up gravel. Immediately, one thing becomes certain: a vehicle is rapidly approaching his driveway.

Not expecting any company, he sits in confusion. With a sarcastic snicker, he shakes his head in disbelief and shifts his cupped hand to rub his ear neurotically.

He loathes surprises, and the thought of his schedule being interrupted escalates his anxiety. To curb his angst, he neurotically chuckles and gazes at Olive, nuzzled in his lap. "You hear that, girl? Sounds like a car. I'm not sure about you, but I don't remember inviting over any guests," he says.

Olive tilts her snout up and loudly oinks. Her response strikes a nerve in Tom, and he glares down at her with suspicion. "Did you invite company over behind my back? Are you hiding something from me?" he asks.

The sound of the car's brakes screeching to a stop outside causes his heartbeat to quicken. Something isn't right; each of the sow's typically endearing oinks, when paired with the shrill sound of the bone-dry car door hinges opening, heckles his ears.

An intense ringing resonates in his skull as he fixates on the booted footsteps approaching the barn. The appearance of his once-pleasant expression drastically shifts. Unable to tolerate the sensory overload, the weight on his lap sends him over the edge, and with a forceful heave, he shoves Olive off his legs. "Get off me, you deceitful bitch!" Olive releases a high-pitched squeal, running to join the rest of the herd.

Springing to his feet, Tom clutches his hair between his fists, trying to make the noise stop. He takes a deep breath, and his hands gradually release their grip, leaving each palm holding a chunk of hair ripped from its roots.

The terrified squeals of his favorite pig make his stomach drop. While firmly squinching his eyes shut, he desperately waves his hand toward the crying animals. "I'm sorry, I didn't mean that. I love you more than anything. You know I wouldn't hurt you," he says as he stumbles toward them.

The untreated hinges of the large barn door release an agonizing screech as it opens. A sudden flood of bright light from the outside world forces itself inside the darkened habitat. Unaccustomed to the excessive sunlight, Tom's focus shifts to the excruciating pain of the daylight rays blinding his eyes. The unbearable stinging sensation stops him dead in his tracks, and his hands flail to shield his sensitive corneas.

Continuing its momentum, the barn door slides open the rest of the way, and a brief silence falls over the scene.

A wave of confidence flows through Tom's body as he prepares to confront the intruder, and with all his might, he squints his eyes to see who it is, but the sun's harsh illumination casts a blinding glare that hides the man's identity. Something seems familiar. The distinct imagery reminds Tom of a specific memory he has neglected to recall since his youth.

He and his mother often played games incorporating hiding in dark closets to escape his belligerent father's wrath. Toward the end of his time with her, the routine became so normalized that he vaguely recollects the terror of his father's backlit image and its debilitating effects.

The memory makes his confidence crumble. Just as fast as it arrived, the power leaves his limbs, and, trying to muster up enough courage, his dry lips attempt to part to speak, but they refuse.

Without missing a beat, the mysterious figure steps inside the barn, and the heels of his cowboy boots click against the concrete floor. The sound causes Tom to flinch.

Even though the figure is silent, he exudes undeniably boisterous male energy as his lungs break the stagnancy of speech with a loud hack. His hand waves in front of his nose. "Woo-wee, its sure smells like a sack of shit in here, don't it?" he says.

Tom pays close attention to the voice's timbre. It sounds nothing like the memories he has of his older man. In response to the discovery, his reaction drastically shifts, and the memory of his past trauma dissipates. Internally dwelling on the man's rudeness, his posture straightens, and fists clench by his sides.

The stranger steps further inside the barn. He takes his sweet time making his way to the fence of the hog pen as his eyes run over the scenery. Tom's knuckles turn a hue of white as they clench tighter. "Who are you? What do you want?"

The piercing tone of his voice throws off the visitor. Resting his hands against the metal rails of the pen, he leans his weight evenly on his palms, doing a double take at Tom's appearance. "What in God's green earth happened to you?" he asks as his glance moves over the cluster of pigs. "You are looking no better than them."

Tom takes a moment to analyze each detail of the rude man's slovenly appearance. His shrunken white tank top covered in moth-bitten holes doesn't cover the entirety of his beer gut. The hair on his head is sparse, comprising only a few dyed black strands combed over an expansive bald spot. A pair of dirty loose-fitting jeans sits midway on his pelvic bone, secured with a worn black leather belt and tarnished brass buckle in the shape of a pig's face, with the initials D. B. below the carving. The dull nature of the metal matches the dirt-ridden gray cowboy boots sticking out from below his pant legs.

"That's no way to treat a customer now, is it?" the man asks.

Tom casually shrugs. "I like to know who's on my property. My mechanic shop is closed 'til a day shy of mid-month, so I wasn't expecting any customers," he says. "You're showing up outside business hours and without an appointment. It caught me off-guard."

The stranger looks at Tom dead center in his pupils with an intimidating squint. "Hmm. I see," he says. The man runs his tongue over the flat fronts of his teeth, causing his cheeks to make a high-pitched suction sound. He licks his index finger and polishes his belt buckle. "D.B. is short for Danny Boy," he says with a sarcastic smile. "You must be Tom."

Never having seen his face before or heard of the man, Tom's mind grows flustered over the fact that Danny Boy knows his identity. The muscles in his neck tighten around his jugular as he takes a deep gulp. "That's a nice buckle you got," Tom says.

Danny shifts his weight between his cowboy boots and puffs out his chest. "Are you staring at my crotch?" he asks.

Tom rapidly shakes his head. "No... No, I just like pigs, that's all. They are beautiful creatures."

Breaking his composure, Danny laughs uncontrollably. His boisterous hysterics rumble between the tin walls like a canned thunderstorm, sending the pigs into a squealing frenzy. Tom swiftly covers his ears to shield himself from the chaos. "Stop it! You are upsetting them!" he desperately shouts.

Finding the man's neurotic behavior funny, he continues his torment by deliberately reaching for the pigpen's entrance. "Last time I checked, it was a free country, Tom, and I can laugh if I want to."

His eyes glance down at Tom, sitting among the herd of pigs in the middle of the pen's dirt floor, and wanting to provoke a further rise out of him, he grabs hold of the gate and shakes it. The momentum of the heavy chain striking the corroded metal bars produces a nerve-racking clank.

Danny spots Tom flinching and cruelly shakes the gate again. "I'm not here for your mechanical services, Tom," he says with a wide smile. "No, siree. I am here on account of hearing there was a fresh challenger in town planning to enter a pig into the annual pig jamboree."

His eyes drift from Tom to his prized belt buckle. Using the bottom of his tank top, he stretches the material to polish the brass-coated metal. "This little thing right here doesn't mean I'm second or third place. It means I'm a winner, and that's that. So, you can imagine the feeling I got when a little bird told me a new fella had a good-looking pig entering this year's shindig."

Shifting his attention, he flips his wrist to point to the herd. "But, by the look of things, I have nothing to worry about." Finished with his provocation, he laughs and whimsically pivots on his boots' heels to face the exit's direction.

Tom bends at the waist to slow his hyperventilation, and upon catching his breath, a spurt of courage fills his gut. He mutters, "You better never say a word about my pigs again."

Hearing the response, Danny stops mid-step. "What did you say, boy?" he asks.

Tom rises to his feet, and his posture straightens. A bead of sweat rolls down his forehead and lands in the crease of his pursed lips. "I—I said you better never talk about my pigs like that again," he says.

Danny charges the gate to intimidate him and hits the adjoining post with his fist. "Or what?" he asks. "What would a pussy of a man like you do to a well-hung man like me?"

With a giant gulp and gritted teeth, Tom takes a huge step forward. Cheering squeals sound behind him, and their encouragement causes his voice to grow louder. "I'll let them have you," he says as his hands drop to his sides.

Danny has never had someone stand up to him before. The novelty of Tom's threat lights a fire under the seat of Danny's trousers. Running out of insults, he grasps for low jabs to bully him further. "You know, you kind of walk like a female," he says while he fumbles to unchain the gate. "Wait 'til I get in there, little girl. You're gonna regret the day you were born."

Tom stands his ground as he watches him enter the pig pen. "My pinky is more of a man than you," Danny says. Less than a foot away from each other, their height discrepancy becomes blatantly apparent.

Danny smiles while staring directly at him as he reaches to unbuckle his belt. "You willing to bet your manhood on it?" he says. His fingers move toward his pants' silver buttons. After a moment of fumbling, he becomes frustrated and glances down to obtain a better view to speed up the process.

The pig's squeals become so shrill that they resemble the sound of human screams. At the height of the animal's distress, Tom notices the makeshift rope halter used to lead Olive over the fence's corner ledge. Thinking on his feet, he sprints to grab it.

Noticing the building angst in the barn, Danny's large fingers fumble quicker to undo his pants' remaining buttons. "Don't you dare go anywhere! I'm not done with you, twinkle toes," he says as a hardening bulge protrudes from the crotch of his jeans. His mouth grins as the last button releases and the pressure against his scrotum lifts.

Danny's eyes rise, and he intently scans the pen for his prey. As he opens his mouth to call for Tom, a startling force constricting his esophagus cuts his words short. Unsure what is happening, his arms flail wildly toward his neck, and his pants drop to the floor.

Every muscle in Tom's face clenches with intensity as he stands behind Danny, rope lead in hand, and, with each choking gasp, he pulls the rope tighter around his neck. Watching the grown man's knees buckle brings him a sense of power, and the testosterone surge causes his voice to deepen. "Who's afraid now?" he says with a cynical laugh. "My pigs are my business, you understand me?" he screams.

Not hearing a response, anger fills him, causing him to jerk the makeshift noose violently. Danny, gagging and in a state of delirium from the lack of oxygen, stumbles, his feet fumbling underneath him, entangled in the wadded pile of stiff jean material resting around his ankles.

Sensing his body losing balance, Tom releases the rope. As the man tumbles to the ground, his skull catches the edge of the concrete slab. The forceful impact creates a bone-chilling crack like the sound of a fallen tree. Though unresponsive, blood flows from D.B.'s mouth, ears, and eyes in pulsing streams, indicating his heart's sustained viability.

Tom unemotionally approaches Danny's twitching body and stands over him. His eyes gravitate to the shiny belt buckle on the jeans bunched around his tormentor's ankles. Leaning over, he grabs the belt and unsnaps the brass sculpture of the pig from the leather.

Danny's fingers twitch as his dilating pupils shift to look in Tom's direction. He attempts to speak, but rather than disgorging vile words; he only spews blood.

Tom ignores the dying man, fixated solely on the belt buckle's glory. "Looks like there's gonna be a new pig king in town," he says as he wipes a crimson droplet from the item's gold-tinged snout. He moves it closer to his face to study the engraved lettering. "Don't worry, D.B.; it shouldn't be too hard to give this thing the initials of its rightful owner: me."

Tom removes the rope from Danny's neck, lays it back over the fence, exits the pen, and locks the gate behind him. He smirks as he makes eye contact with the throng of pigs circling the man in the dirt. "Go on, now! It's feeding time!"

Their squeals turn to shrieks of excitement as they swarm his flinching body and, in a frenzy, begin devouring every sinewy bite, clothes, bones, and all.

Knowing he must hide the prized buckle somewhere for safekeeping, he opens a rickety wooden cabinet that houses the pigs' grooming supplies and tucks it away behind a brush. He recognizes that the pigs have performed enough work for the day, so he allows them to rest.

As he makes his way to the open sliding door of the barn, he whistles to the tune of Old McDonald. His lips can't help smiling at the sounds of bones crunching between the livestock's teeth, and the addition of the sun's warmth against his skin as he steps outside makes the moment even more perfect.

Tom approaches Danny's truck parked in the barnyard, and it relieves him to find the keys still in the ignition. He chuckles as he drives it into the overgrown wooded area that marks the property's edge and, with some careful maneuvering, perfectly stows it out of sight.

Chapter Five
SURE, A PRETTY PIG

Tom's encounter with the foul intruder has offered him a new lease on life. Rather than cling to the trauma of the precarious situation, he shrugs it off as nothing out of the ordinary. To him, it isn't worth the slightest moment of reflection. He knows if he compares it to any of his childhood memories in the foster care system, it will present as trivial, and the time squandered contrasting the two would merely provoke anger.

The only relevancy he finds from the grotesque interaction with the man is his delight when admiring the ornate belt buckle. Day after day, his fondness for the newly gained possession grows, and he soon becomes consumed by its intricacies. He lies awake night after night, pondering the time it took the designer to style each tiny groove of the swine's refined details, and can't help fixating on the day he will display it between his hipbones.

Tom has an epiphany: what better time to unveil his new good-luck charm than at the approaching jamboree, but first, he must make it his own.

He remembers his grandfather's rickety old drill press hidden in the barn's corner. Moth-bitten gunny sacks drape over the top, making it inconspicuous. Tom cleans off the cobwebs, drags the device to a nearby wall outlet, and plugs it in. When switched on, it hums like new, surprisingly. An old c-clamp mounted to the equipment tabletop proves perfect for stabilizing the piece so he can drill further detail into the metal.

With a hammer in one hand and a rusted chisel in the other, he taps away, day and night, morphing the buckle into a sow resembling his dearest love, Olive. It is the only thing he finds worthy of taking precious time away from his cloven-hoofed family. The most important thing to him is fashioning a perfect likeness. He even taps into his creative side by adding a frilly bow to the top of her head, right between her ears. Once content with the resemblance, he migrates his attention to the initials below Olive's tiny dainty feet.

Tom uses every tool available to obscure any sign of the previous owner's identity. In its place, his internal anger shows through his hand's pressure, and he creates deep etches of three letters to flaunt his first name: Tom.

The sight of the new engraving puts a soft twinkle in the dull whites of his irises, and the warm sensation of the worked metal against his calloused fingertips makes a win feel within his grasp. Tom is confident that simply brushing his fingertips against the face of the buckle brings him good fortune, making it impossible to lose when Olive steps into the sawdust ring and makes her debut in the community.

He snickers at the image of the work of art adorning his pelvis as he proudly struts around the competition ring. The belts sheen will put all eyes on him, and for once, the thought of becoming the talk of the town pleases him.

Every day that creeps closer to the infamous July twelfth date builds a sense of anxiety in the barn's stagnant air. Like a persistent tick, it pulls any sense of relaxation from Tom's veins and kills any potential for rest from his recurrent sleepless nights. He becomes jittery, and all outside stimuli provoke an abnormal startled reaction, no matter how routine the noise may be.

As insomnia affects his outward appearance, dark circles develop beneath the reds of his sleep-deprived eyes. He is exhausted and finds that the only way to wake himself up each morning is the unpleasant sensation of ice-cold water against his skin.

He starts his day by submerging his head in the pig trough's frigid water, and as his mental state worsens, he repeats the uncomfortable cycle every hour on the hour.

With his insomnia, as he lies next to the pigs each night, his restless mind obsesses over every possible idiosyncrasy that could reveal itself on Olive's body. After they wake, he searches for defects in her skin while giving her a morning bath. Then, to ease the chance of surprise notes of criticism from the jamboree judges, he makes mental notes about any validated flaws.

At the edge of his breaking point, his eyes remain peeled open as the daylight touches the sky on the twelfth of July. Unable to attain an ounce of shut-eye, Tom sits alone in silence on his makeshift mattress of hay in the pen's corner, dwelling on every detail of his surroundings.

The pile of pigs is sound asleep. His crazed stare fixates on their snoring snouts, and the view of their peaceful, picturesque appearances makes him smile. Knowing he is the only one privy to their carnivorous secrets gives him a sick sense of self-importance.

Basking in his moment of reflection, he turns to face the breach in the barn's wall to watch the sunrise take shape. Minute by minute, hues of orange and pink pastels peek through the peeling edges of the tin. Then, remaining dead still, he holds his breath, waiting for a single ray of light to caress his pale skin, signaling that it is time to begin preparation for the big day.

Unable to sustain his patience any longer, his body springs to stand, and his arms stretch up into the sky, elongating his spine. He lets out a long yawn, and his feet carry him across the packed dirt toward the pig trough. Even though he is impatient to use a splash of water to awaken his mind, he takes a moment, hovering above the liquid to observe his reflection. While analyzing his appearance, he inhales a long, deep breath through his nostrils, and as he exhales the air between his lips, his finger points at his likeness. "You are a winner. Don't let anyone tell you differently," he says.

Each affirmation cuts through the early morning air, and the words' vibrations tickle inside the canals of the sleeping pigs' ridged ears. As if reacting to a siren's call, their stiff bodies leisurely roll over in their groggy state, bumping into one another. Their ears flutter as they attempt to stop the itching sensation. Still disturbed by the noise, they wake with a few gentle snorts.

Olive lies at the edge of the group. One by one, her legs stretch, locking straight in front of her to relieve the pressure from her back. Her snout wiggles as movement stirs within the muscles of her face.

The sounds of the herd awakening break Tom's gaze upon his reflection, and his eyes close as his ears enjoy the lively tune from the creatures. The immersive experience causes affection to fill his chest cavity, and without turning around, he joins in by humming a good morning melody.

The animals grow louder, chiming in with invigorated squeals. Tom revels in the tune as each unique voice builds in enthusiasm.

His eyes remain closed, his chin tilts, and his shoulders bounce as a jittery sensation travels up his torso, releasing a boisterous round of unrestrained laughter. Then, further breaking the silence, he clears his throat to speak. "Good morning, everyone! Can you believe today is the big day?" he asks.

The hogs squeal gleefully. Tom's eyes spring open at the onslaught of loving calls, and an unexpected scene meets his gaze.

A crowd of individuals oddly clusters near the grain bin just beyond the fence.

Tom's eyes glance from left to right. Even though their bodies' translucent nature makes it clear they are apparitions, his mind doesn't make the distinction between living and dead. They all appear normal to him. Having no recollection of seeing anyone when he initially made his way to the watering hole floods him with confusion.

Tom's anxiety takes hold, and he freezes in place. His mind races as if waiting for them to cast the wrath of judgment.

The crowd chats among themselves. Their voices unify pitch, tone, and tempo, mimicking an eerie chant.

Two familiar faces—his grandparents, Earl and Bertha—emerge from the crowd and make their way to the front of the group. The sole attribute that signifies their demise is the ashen skin covering their frail bones. All their lacerations, bludgeoning, and ligature wounds are gone. Although it appears they wish to speak, their silence contradicts their assertive movement forward.

Tom can't contain his growing curiosity. Even though crowds of people overwhelm his senses, he still finds something inside of him drawn to the unfolding scene. His eyes squint, focusing on his grandparents' faces while noticing that they appear rather typical. Bewildered by the image, he fumbles for words to solve the mystery of what has healed them. "Did you make a pact with the devil or something?" he asks.

Their lack of dismemberment causes him a sick sense of disappointment. It almost takes away a piece of validation and camaraderie he shares with his pigs.

The crowd's words are indecipherable to him, but the herd's awe-like expressions indicate that they understand the babbling.

Tom suddenly realizes the large group's presence has yet to stir panic in him. The unusual sense of calm is abnormal, and he determines that his grandparents' company must have something to do with it. His profound annoyance toward them seems to divert his attention away from his usual episodes of social anxiety.

With a slight smirk, he nervously lifts his right palm and bends each boney finger to wave at the couple. The action triggers the muscles in his grandparents' faces to abruptly go limp, drooping their skin like melting wax.

Tom's hand pauses as he stares wide-mouthed in a state of confusion. Mesmerized by their repulsive appearance, he admires them like an abstract piece of art. He glances at his hand with amazement and wonders if his fingers hold an essence of magic, like conductors of a morbid puppet show.

Wanting to test his suspicion, he returns his attention to the assembly. Unfortunately, the bystanders behind the elderly couple are oblivious to the exchange and remain unchanged by Tom's digits movements as they continue their fixation on the group of pigs behind him.

Static fills the air from the entities' energy, causing the pigs' hair to stand on end and their agitated bodies to roam the pen. The spectacle of aimlessly wandering animals entertains the crowd, and they clap to exude praise for Tom's award-winning herd.

Tom's stomach clenches, and a sense of paranoia squeezes his rib cage as he gawps at the throng with a dumbfounded look. As his mind stirs to grasp what is causing his discomfort, the elderly couple eerily tilts their heads to mirror his movement while they mockingly return his gawking stare.

Their mouths gape open, exposing discolored dentures as their lungs release a raspy breath. The whites of their eyes turn mustard-yellow, and their pupils expand to the corners of their wrinkled lids. The expression is hard to interpret as it conveys a strange mix of loathing, anger, sadness, and surprise. Nothing about their appearance or disjointed facial movements makes sense, and Tom finds their presence and his inability to decipher their true intentions unnerving.

Suddenly, his ears are overcome by an annoying buzzing sound, much like a swarm of mosquitoes, and he panics. His limbs become petrified, unable to move.

Ever since childhood, he has had an extreme phobia of insects flying into his ears, crawling to the furthest point of their canals, burrowing into his brain, and controlling his thoughts. Typically, he covers his ear holes when the fear arises, but he cannot move his hands to protect himself.

Sweat drips from his forehead as his body tenses. His pupils wildly scan the crowd to identify the sound's origin, concluding that it stems from his grandmother's esophagus.

Bertha recognizes his habitual fixation and devilishly expels a loud hack to clear her lungs. A commotion stirs around her uvula, dangling in the back of her throat. Then, in a single whoosh, a swarm of horseflies clouds the space in front of her gaping mouth and flaring nostrils.

The buzzing horde sweeps through the air toward Tom at the speed of light. Slowing to a snail's pace, they torment him by hovering in front of his eyes for what seems like a lifetime before torpidly circling his head. Their wings vibrate, loudly buzzing while brushing against his ears as they pass. Then, without notice, they fly away and funnel between the gap in Earl's parted lips.

After disappearing into Earl's mouth, his bulging Adam's Apple tracks their journey as he swallows, forcing each fly into the pit of his stomach.

The elderly couple takes a split-second pause, and then, without looking at one another, they point at Tom in unison and repeat, "Murderer, murderer, murderer, murderer, murderer..."

Tom's mind begins an internal fight to free the vertebrae in his neck to allow his head to shake in denial. His jaw tightens in preparation to spew words to defend himself, and the force of his attempt creates a harsh tone as he shouts, "No!"

The sound of his rebellion further provokes Earl and Bertha, who shift their voices to a more antagonistic tenor while refusing to break their intimidating stares. The crowd joins in as they continue their heckling. "Murderer, murderer, murderer," they repeat.

Tom's skull aches as the words reverberate and madden him like a jagged nail running down a schoolroom chalkboard. The accusations resonate

between his ears as the taunting increasingly etches into his brain.

Without warning, a sheet of darkness descends
over him, and in unison, his body frees from its
paralyzed state.

Terrified of losing control, he tries to fight the
feeling by hunching forward and clutching his
hair. As his fingers intertwine with the greasy
strands, he pulls with all his might, lifting his scalp
from his skull.

His attempt to inflict enough pain to distract
him from his rising anger proves futile, and, having
no luck, he refocuses his attention on the buzzing
noise still tormenting his mind. "Shut up!" he says.

Every sound he had wished to silence produces
a crescendo that drowns out his plea. Feeding into
the mayhem, his grandparents continue their stare
while the crowd's heckling chants fall out of sync.

Tom scans each set of beady pupils to distinguish
who has caused the mismatched rhythm, and the
sight of their soulless disregard thrusts him into
an emotional meltdown. His eyelids close to escape
their judgmental gawping as his inner core fills
with conflict.

A rush of sadness warps his strength, dropping
him to a crouch on the ground. He struggles to up-
hold the mental stability he has worked tirelessly
to maintain, and his weakness creates a deep sense
of loathing.

With an expression simulating a victim's, he
peers at his grandparents, hoping to incite any

sign of compassion. "I just wanted to make you proud!" he says.

Emotionless, they stare back at him, and he finds nothing is working to relieve him from the demons that haunt him.

The indifferent reaction causes his body to become weak, and his cheeks burn from the heat of his simmering anger. Finally, tired of fighting to suppress his rage, he allows it to take over and guide his actions. "Why are you doing this to me? Wasn't your abandonment enough!" he asks angrily.

The pigs' squeals grow louder behind him. It's past the usual time of their morning meal, and they have become agitated.

The high-pitched shrieks from the crying pigs match the grandparent's and crowd's condemnations, morphing together to create a deafening shrill. "Killer, murderer, killer!" they say.

Tom cannot decipher where the voices end and the pigs begin. As his emotions spiral, his heart palpitations surge, and he frantically fumbles to carry on his routine, aware of how fast the progression can turn into full-blown debilitating hysteria.

He knows it is the only hope left. He must ground himself.

Bertha and Earl have him where they want him, and the corners of their open mouths smirk. "Die, die, die. You will die, just like I!" they say.

Tom winces from the pain resonating in his skull. Moving his hands from his hair, he places them on each side of the water trough's edge to stabilize his weakening knees, then hinges forward at his hip to catch his breath.

Without taking a moment of pause, he submerges his head into the pool of cold liquid. As the skin on his face feels like it's being stabbed with millions of ice-laden needles, he screams into the water to make it stop, and bubbles surface.

When he comes up for air, all is silent.

The disturbance is gone.

Tom gives a once-over to the area his grandparents had stood, and his lungs squeeze out a fictitious laugh. As his racing heart calms, he lets down his guard and uses a palm to wipe the water away from his eyes.

One of the roaming pigs snorts a short distance behind him as it searches for food. "I will be with you in a minute, my darlings," Tom says as he dries his face.

The environment in the barn looks to return to normal. Tom uses his fists to vigorously rub his eyes and uses the momentary darkness to help himself regain control.

Without warning, something brushes against his right earlobe, stiffening the hairs on the back of his neck. His body jumps upon sensing someone beside him. Tom's eyelids remain closed underneath his fingers while his hands tremble against his cheekbones.

A puff of warm air forms a single word. "Killer!" it says.

Tom's eyes spring open with terror, and every bone in his body freezes. His stark panic causes his legs to go numb and his stance to wobble. As the blood flow flushes from his legs, he places his hands on his thighs to prevent his body from buckling, and his kneecaps quiver under his clenched palms. His heart races, and each beat grows louder.

Then, as if acting on impulse, his upper body snaps up to stare in the voice's direction.

Nothing is there.

The pigs root through the dirt floor, searching for food, ignorant of his mental despair. Tom grows paranoid over their calm behavior.

A bead of sweat drips into his eyes, and he is so overwhelmed by his turmoil that he doesn't flinch from the sting.

Olive smells the salt exuding from his perspiring skin. As she lifts her snout from the dirt, she takes notice of his shaking limbs, and, sensing his distress, she strays away from the group to make her way toward him.

Tom's gaze remains straight ahead, locked on discovering the origin of the phantom voice.

Olive brushes her body against his leg to get his attention. The unexpected weight hitting near the back of his knee almost knocks him over, and thinking it is associated with the heckling, Tom is ready to fight. His fists clench as he scans the area for the cause.

Olive's concerned eyes meet his, and his mind calms. His lips loosen to form a smile. She wiggles her nose to lift her upper lip and shows her teeth.

Tom reaches down to pet her. As he opens his mouth to speak, the skittishness of his reaction creates a stutter, and fighting through his embarrassment, he chuckles. "The lack of sleep must be getting to me, ole girl," he says. She nuzzles his leg and releases a few oinking sounds.

Tom attempts to pretend everything is okay, but something doesn't feel right inside him. He can't find the truth within the assurance he had given Olive, and his thoughts continue to run wild behind his smile. As the lingering ache of his upset stomach persists, Tom puts on a brave face to hush his internal discourse. He reluctantly lifts his hand from her back and turns around to finish his morning routine. Tom scoops water with his hands, haphazardly washing the essential parts of his body underneath his dirty clothes.

Each splashing sound reminds Olive of her soothing baths, and she scoots closer to Tom.

The small sounds from her snorting snout are soothing to his mind, and he smiles. "It will be your turn next," he says as he finishes washing. Then, cupping water in his palms, he kneels next to Olive and runs the liquid through the fur on her back.

She squeals with happiness, and as the liquid cools her skin, her backside wiggles with glee. Tom ogles her curly pink tail with endearment.

"That's my little star," he says, scooping another handful of water.

Then, he begins aggressively rubbing the dull-colored fur on her body, scrubbing more thoroughly than usual. "You must be perfect." His hand's zealous movement against Olive's delicate skin creates a burning sensation, and she cringes to show her discomfort.

Tom's obsession with winning takes over his mind and nothing else in the room matters. Paying no care to her signs of discomfort, he ignores her facial cues and rubs harder. He falls into an obsessive trance focused only on making her coat as shiny as possible.

Olive squeals at the top of her lungs and bares her teeth to nip at him.

The harsh sound of her snapping molars brings him back to reality, and his hand abruptly retracts from her body as if pulling away from the smacking jaws of a crocodile. Realizing she is in pain, he frantically apologizes, "I'm so... so sorry, Olive. I'm sorry. I didn't mean to hurt you."

Unable to look her in the eyes, he glances down at the clumps of her hair in his palms and desperately attempts to brush them off. The horrifying sight of strands cascading to the dirt causes his fingers to tremble. As he analyzes the fur on the floor, he worries that his zealous actions have created a bald spot on her back that will cause a deduction in the judge's score. Tom, faced with his greatest fear, warily scans her spine, but the sight leaves him confused.

Rather than a bald area of irritated, raw pink skin, a patch of golden fur sits in its place. The brilliant color of the new luscious strands of hair is exquisite in appearance.

The mesmerizing sight causes Tom's brows to furrow as he flounders for an explanation.

Olive wants to see what is drawing his focus. Her neck kinks as she tries to examine her back, and her mouth salivates. The foreign patch of fur has a straw-like resemblance, and like a hungry hippo, she snaps her mouth at the area for a taste, but her head cannot reach it.

From his frozen entrancement over the radiant hair, Tom motions for her to stop and scratches his chin to ponder how the lush locks came about. "What the..." he says. Taking a moment, he wipes the residual strands of Olive's long coarse hair from his palms onto his pants. Still, in disbelief, he covers his eyes to take a moment to think. He cautiously peeks between his fingers to take a second look and to see if the phenomenon remains.

A small gust of wind squeezes through the breach in the barn's tin siding, and the infiltrating humid air delicately ruffles her gilded strands like fingers sifting through a treasure chest of gold coins.

Each follicle's slow dancing motion showcases Olive's extraordinary undercoat's rich hue's beauty, and Tom sees the potential for cold hard cash. In his mind, he has stumbled upon the motherload.

As he smiles from ear to ear, a gritty scream exits his mouth to show the world his excitement. Lunging forward, he tackles Olive's body and latches onto her torso. His head burrows into the patch of bright fur, and the strands gently caress his cheek. "I always knew you were special," he says.

Even though Olive's new patch of hair is lush, the skin underneath remains tender to the touch, and the squeeze of his embrace causes her to flinch. The abruptness of her shifting body weight makes him worry she may try to run away, and in response, he tightens his hands around her belly so that she cannot move.

Tom briefly looks at her face to simulate a flash of empathy, but the moment is short-lived. Before Olive can lock eyes with him, he repositions himself on top of her, pinning her to the floor, and like a maniac, wildly begins rubbing every inch of her body.

A burning pain overtakes Olive, and she cries, unable to escape the heat of the unbearable friction. Every one of her atrocious squeals is unlike anything Tom has heard before, and they cause his forehead to accumulate sweat. As her body continues to squirm, the thought of losing control and frustration over the situation flushes his skin with an angry red. "Stop moving, you bitch!" he says as he struggles to keep her submissive.

He watches her shedding coat tumble to the dirt and lush new golden hair replace each missing strand—his hands dash to finish the job.

Olive's pleading screams worsen, and though he attempts to sympathize with her sacrifice, he can no longer keep his composure and wants her to experience how annoying she is. Firing back at her loud eruption, he shouts straight into her ear, matching the provoking tone of her shriek.

Olive revolts and fights to get away. Tom's approach becomes more forceful, and his hands more aggressive. "Stop it; I'm helping you!" he says as he strikes her rib cage with a fist.

What he once considered an act of compassion takes a cynical turn into a punishing lesson. Shocked by his outburst, he backtracks, and his voice softens, "I didn't... I mean, I don't want to hurt you. You know I'm not violent. If you just listened, none of this would have happened."

Still upset by the treatment, Olive digs her nose into the ground to hide her tearing eyes and sniffling nose.

Pushing past his guilt, Tom finishes rubbing every last untouched inch of her body, and upon completion of his actions, the skin on his palms is left chapped and blistered. Nevertheless, he is satisfied with the result. Olive's fur has transformed from long, dull hair to glistening golden locks.

Tom releases her body to catch his breath and uses his sleeve to wipe the sweat from his brow. As he calms himself, he admires her exotic coat.

His violent nature and inflicted abuse have upset Olive. She sits up, and her snout points to the ground in defeat.

Noticing her stagnancy, Tom tries to force eye contact with her to make things better. He crawls on all fours in her direction, and with a tender touch, he gently lifts the bottom of her chin. He notices a tear in the corner of her eye and affectionately brushes it away. "It's okay, girl. As they say, beauty is pain... I mean, that couldn't have been that bad," he shrugs.

Olive snorts at him. He ignores her disdain as his eyes scan over her lush coat. "My, my, you sure are pretty," he says with a grin.

Giving in to his positive words of affirmation, Olive puffs out her chest and turns up her lips to smile. Tom rubs her ears and notices his plan of excessively complimenting her is working, and her souring mood is dissipating.

As they stare into each other's eyes to share a redeeming moment, nothing else matters but their bonding time together.

That is until a loud, heinous screech sounds from across the room.

Olive's ears stand straight up to listen to the uncomfortable echo bouncing between the tin walls.

Tom's mind is flustered as her attentiveness diverts away from him. Not wanting their moment to end, he reluctantly glances up to see what has caught her attention and spots the sliding barn door starting to open.

"Knock, knock," a woman calls from outside the barn. "Yoo-hoo! Your chauffeur is here!" The bubbly high-pitched tone makes it clear that she is a morning person.

Before giving anyone time to respond, she continues, "I'm just kidding! It's me, Claudia!" Her drawn-out laughter suggests that she thinks she is funnier than the sight of a tiny car stuffed with a dozen clowns.

Still struggling to gather his bearings from his brief breakdown, Tom finds the woman's voice a bit much. Regardless of his irritation, his mind focuses just enough to associate the familiar speech pattern with the name, and he connects the dots.

One thing that startles him after catching sight of the sun's glare through the thin gap in the door is how much time has already slipped away. Frantically, he glances at piles of hair scattering the pen's dirt floor, and, realizing how bad the situation may appear to an onlooker, he panics.

He quickly springs to his feet and brushes himself off.

The sound of the barn door's screeching slows, and Tom is sure that the greaseless track is the cause of her delayed entrance, buying him a bit of time.

Olive watches in confusion as he rushes around the pen like a madman, stirring up dust clouds while kicking each pile of hair to disperse the evidence.

The heavy barn door rollers hit a snag, and it refuses to budge. Claudia vehemently shoves the unruly object and becomes frustrated that the act is causing her to perspire. Attempting to maintain her dignity, she focuses on preserving her lady-like composure and short-fused temper, but the door's stubbornness gets to her.

Unable to keep up her facade, her lips utter an enormous grunt. The complexion of her skin flushes with embarrassment over her release of the unappealing sound.

She wants nothing more than to see into the barn, but the crack is too small to accommodate her head. Though frustrated, she momentarily sees it as an advantage since Tom could not see her through the tiny opening, making it easy for her to pretend not to have been the one that made the noise.

She pushes on the rebellious door while covering up her irritation with short bursts of giggles.

Finally, she creates a big enough crack to poke her head inside. "Coming!" she sings in a melodic tone with a hint of vibrato.

The pigs respond to her call with laugh-like squeals, chiming in like a choir to her melody.

Claudia renounces the idea that the heavy door's stubbornness will win. Instead of focusing on a different approach, she pushes forward, refusing to let the minor snafu cramp the style of her entrance.

Eyeing the width of the opening and turning sideways, she tries to remain endearing while shimmying herself through the narrow passage.

Tom's short attention span has already kicked in by the midpoint of her struggles, and he has long succumbed to his boredom regarding her entrance. Unbothered by her or what she is doing, his gaze returns to the texture of Olive's lush fur coat. He can't take his eyes off the vibrant, hypnotizing color.

As she finishes squeezing through the crack of an entrance, her sideways position reveals a small pastry box clutched beneath her arm. Claudia stares at the door with a stern glare and half-jokingly pats its tin shell to show it who's boss.

Despite pretending she doesn't exist, Tom winces at her noisy arrival while remaining engaged in a world that only involves Olive.

Claudia, too, remains in a different world, but it's smaller; it only involves her.

Clearing her throat, she lets out a mismatched cackle. "You sure are a stubborn one, just like your grandaddy."

Awkwardly dragging out her laughter, her eyes scan the barn, and she attempts to fill the air with small talk to capture Tom's attention. "I brought donuts from a local baker in town. Well, I guess the only baker in town. You know, everyone who's anyone has been talking about them, so I thought—"

Stopping mid-speech, she gasps at the sight of Olive's lush golden locks. Her hand bolts to clutch her heart, and the box underneath her arm falls, scattering the cake donuts across the dirty concrete floor.

The pigs' excitement escalates over the smell of cinnamon-dusted dough, and the commotion catches Tom's attention. He turns just in time to see donuts rolling in every direction.

He is oblivious to the woman's stunned expression, focusing solely on the details of her clothing rather than her face.

Claudia has dressed for the day's occasion. She is wearing a flouncy dress that stops just below the knee. The bottom of the skirt's pale-white eyelet ruffles showcases the material's pattern of pink pigs with chocolate-color spots sprinkling the entire dress from her neck to the top of her calves. Completing the unique ensemble is a scarf crafted from the same fabric, folded into a triangle, holding back the jostled golden-blond pin-curls from her face. Her cheeks and lip color mimic the herd's rosy, pink snouts, and she wears a pair of red Mary Janes with two-inch heels that *clip-clop* as she makes her way across the hard floor.

The pigs depicted on her clothing put a smile on Tom's face and plant seeds of infatuation in his heart. He can't take his eyes off her body, which makes him nervous, and he stammers, "I sure... sure like that dress you have on there."

Usually, Claudia grabs any attention she can get, but Olive's appearance baffles her. Still trying to wrap her mind around the pig's golden glow, his compliment puts her flirtation on overdrive. Squinting her eyes, she glances down at her skirt and, with a neurotic giggle, pretends to listen. "Oh, my, this old thing?" she asks, grabbing the bottom of her dress and spinning. Each swishing movement makes the pigs look like they are dancing. The skirt's motion puts a twinkle in Tom's eye.

As Claudia stops her spin, she wastes no time dashing to the edge of the pen's fence with a playful skip. Tom finds her swift approach, paired with the clicking of her shoes against the concrete, appealing to his senses. He falls into a daze, moving toward the gate, drawn to her like a firefly to a flashlight.

The sight of him approaching feeds Claudia's ego, and she is smitten with the fact that he is taking the initiative. It causes a burst of energy to come over her, and, wanting to keep him engaged, she points to one of the spotted pigs on the front of her dress, directly below her cleavage. She giggles, pretending to be naive about her selection.

Oblivious to the strategic positioning, Tom can't take his pupils off the details of the animal's facial features and becomes fixated as he tries to compare the image to his pigs, past and present.

Noticing his intensifying stare, Claudia takes a moment to formulate a sneaky way to address the elephant in the room while gazing in unison at the printed fabric. Not wanting to disclose her true intentions, she refrains from glancing at Olive and says. "I chose this one to wear because I thought it looked like Olive."

Tom halfheartedly nods and continues his cerebral comparisons.

Claudia's frustration pulls the rose color from her cheeks as she observes his lack of excitement. She ruminates on the time it had taken to match the material to the aesthetic of his favorite pig, and her irritation takes over. Her head tilts to glare at Olive's new fur, and just as she is about to release her wrath, she remembers her goals and regains her composure.

Still obsessed with the fabric and his pigs' similarities, Tom leans forward, pressing his face against the open squares of the woven wire to admire the other pigs on her skirt. He reaches out to touch them, but as his finger is about to graze the animals' outlines, Claudia's anger overtakes her actions, and with a swift flick of her wrist, she pulls the material just out of his reach.

The abrupt disappearing act confuses Tom, and a dumbfounded expression falls across his face as his hand lingers in the air. He cannot focus on anything else but examining the dress's pigs, and, like a cat playing with a ball of yarn, his eyes dart from side to side, searching for the specific image.

Claudia blatantly ignores the stupidity occurring at her waistline and recognizes what she must do, regardless of her annoyance. With the theatrics of a silent film star, her eyes roll to the ceiling, and a single hand dramatically flops across her forehead, partially shielding her eyes. She prepares her monologue with a somber expression and a giant huff of air. "As we all learn... no matter how hard we try, we can't always be perfect." Her lungs let out a heavy sigh. Taking a pause, she listens for Tom's reply and, hearing only silence, half-heartedly shrugs.

Tom squints, deepening his focus on a specific cloth pig, sure that he is coming close to matching its resemblance to a herd member. Claudia, realizing that nothing is working, and finding herself running out of time, breaks the silence with a sarcastic cackle.

As they engage in her irrelevant laughter, the flailing motion of her hands causes Olive to look from behind Tom's legs. She nudges them apart to obtain a better view, and the material of his pants tickles her nose, causing Olive's snout to release a barrage of sneezes. Claudia seethes inside, convinced that the pigs' interruption is deliberately mocking her.

Olive's uncharacteristic sound draws Tom's concern, and he worries that she has caught a cold. His stare shifts to survey his prized possession, and immediately upon eye contact, goosebumps form on his arms, and he becomes dazed by her golden locks. "Do you notice anything different about her? I mean, what do you think? I think she should get a ribbon, right?" he says.

His words knock Claudia out of her theatrical performance. She has been curious about the drastic change in Olive's appearance but was waiting for him to bring it up. Then, putting games aside, she looks into the pen. Additional rays of light enter the barn through the cracked-open door and illuminate Olive's golden fur, causing it to glimmer like brilliant diamonds. Tom pats Olive's back, nervously waiting for Claudia to respond.

Claudia's eyes water as the stimulating colors causes her pupils to dilate. The sight is so magnificent that she finds herself at a loss for words for the first time in her life. "It... it's beautiful," she says. "How?"

Tom casually shrugs. "Only thing I can think of is a change in diet," he says as his eyes drift to a tiny burgundy stain on the edge of the concrete near the gate.

Claudia doesn't care how the miracle happened, only that it did. She is mesmerized by Olive's fur and believes that she has found both a future husband and a life of riches due to the turn of events. "Well, whatever it is, keep doing it," she says.

With a gaping smile, she leans into the fence to gain a closer look and smells an off-putting odor. She begins sniffing the air to determine its origin and realizes Tom's hygiene is the culprit. She lengthens her smile to mask her disgust. "Once you freshen up, we can get on our way."

He doesn't fully catch on to her passive hint and lifts his arm to smell himself. "I just washed this morning," he says.

Claudia refuses to entertain any excuses and stiffens her approach. "You realize the showman's appearance makes all the difference in the winning selection?" she says.

At once, Tom's face shifts to a look of concern. Claudia is pleased that her new approach is working. She nods toward Olive. "Such a shame. Someone could even have a pig made of gold and lose the championship at the pig jamboree because they didn't take the entire presentation seriously."

The words continue to sink in, and Tom's face becomes pale as he peers at Olive, then back to Claudia. Bothered by the thought of disappointing his favorite pig, he shakes his head. "Well, there's one thing for sure: I wouldn't be able to live with myself if I caused that beautiful creature not to win the prize she deserves," he says.

Claudia nods in agreement. "You are one smart man. I know you won't let us down," she says as her hand reaches out to open the gate. "Now, get your tail moving and get yourself ready."

With a skip in his step, Tom takes the bait and rushes out of the pigpen, leaving the entrance open. He suddenly remembers his good-luck charm and, seeing Claudia is preoccupied with closing the gate, sprints to the grooming cabinet and fetches his hidden buckle.

After placing it in his pocket, he takes a few steps away from the hiding spot and notices the cake donuts scattering the floor. He stops and picks two up. "I'll just be a jiff!" he shouts over his shoulder before shoving the spongy dough in his mouth. Then, with a hefty push, he opens the sliding door further and sprints outside, disappearing into the daylight.

Claudia turns around and shakes her head with a giggle. "Sometimes, you just have to let a man think it's all his idea." Then, walking toward the spilled pastry box, she reaches for a glazed maple donut, picks it up, and exhales a big puff of air to blow the dirt off the frosting.

"Mamma was right about one thing..." Taking her first bite of soft dough, she spots a nearby hay bale and glides toward it. She sits all prim and proper, watching the pigs and chewing with her mouth wide open. "Us women know men better than they know themselves," she says with a shrug.

Then she devours the rest of her baked treat.

Chapter Six

SMALL HICCUPS

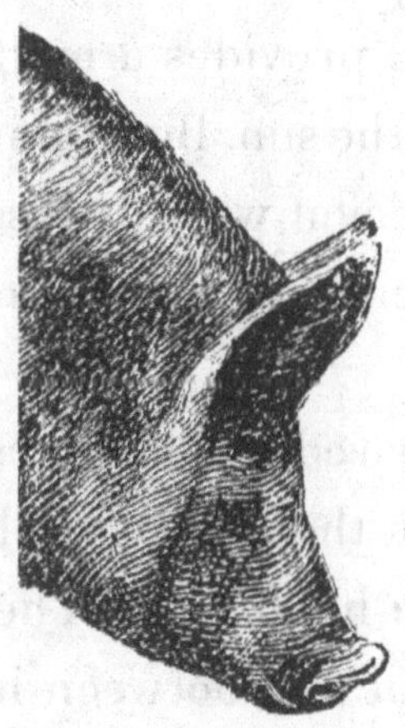

The nonexistent clouds make the sun's iridescent rays more grueling than usual.

Tom places his right hand over his bushy brows to shade his irises from the brightness. With each slow breath he takes to lower his core temperature, his nose fills with a dense heat. Sweat collects on his back, and the oppressive humidity adds unease to his burning lungs. He can't help obsessing over the additional weight holding back his pace, and the feel of the heavy denim sticking to his legs makes him uncomfortable.

It angers him that the extreme elements seem to work against him. *Isn't nature supposed to be relaxing to the nerves?*

As he takes another step, he attempts to dry the damp hairs on his legs by creating airflow with exaggerated kicks of his feet. His lungs release a loud huff as a sign of frustration.

A single cloud provides a momentary layer of protection from the sun. But unfortunately, it only adds to his suspicion when it dissipates from the sky, further unveiling the extent of the harsh rays' potency.

Tom is unprepared for the excessive heat, and it sears the skin on the tops of his hands and forms red splotches on his cheeks. The sloshing liquid rubbing the skin raw between his toes triggers his mind to fixate on the heaviness of his boots. With each of his grueling steps becoming harder to bear, the discomfort of his body picks away at his happiness. Although he is moving, he feels imprisoned, and it causes his anxiety to dig away at his intestines like a shovel cutting through soft soil.

On a bigger mission, he trudges on. At that moment, nothing matters more to him than wanting to honor his queen, which is the most important thing on his mind, and knowing the suffering is for Olive's benefit is enough to keep him sane.

He finds himself contently consumed with the image of her moist nose nuzzling against his skin until the thought of another surprise encounter with his deceased guardians infiltrates his happiness. With the lines of reality blurred, he begins to question if they have taken up residency in the old farmhouse since his relocation to the barn.

Catching himself mid-thought, he chuckles at how crazy the notion is and tries to dispel his silly fear. "They are dead, you old goof," he says as he tilts his head toward the ground and quickens his pace toward the front porch.

A flock of crows caw as they glide through the sky. The sound makes Tom flinch. No matter how much he thinks of Olive, dark underlying emotions surface with each step he takes. Nature's surrounding noises amplify in his ears, and with no way to escape, he feels trapped in a mental prison as he makes his way from the barn to the house.

The sun's blinding rays ricochet off the tiny home's metal gutters and onto the surrounding rural plain. The magnified heat beats down against Tom's vulnerable skin, causing his forehead to drip sweat and the back of his neck to grow tender to the touch. Everything he has worked so hard to suppress is rising to the surface, and he struggles to ignore it.

Since his grandparents' deaths, he has avoided every emotion from the gruesome events conducted within the farmhouse's walls, and to this day, he views retaining the memory as a weakness. Yet, regardless of his wishes, that night continues infiltrating his mind, making one last attempt to fight for control over his thoughts. To stop the spiral, he inhales the remaining squished crumbs of the donut clenched between his fingers.

Tom passes the home's clothesline and sees that, rather than rows of sheets, tiny chirping birds with blue- and red-colored underbellies line the taut wires. A short breeze of warm, humid air blows past him, carrying their chattering conversations through the barnyard. But, rather than soothing, each playful call sounds distorted, like a barn owl screeching when eviscerating its prey.

All Tom can think about is the selfishness of the birds and how they are purposely contributing to the chaos that ruins his life.

Not used to seeing people outside, the birds are startled by Tom's presence and fly away. Their flapping wings create small bursts of wind, reminiscent of the sound of whiffle balls traveling through the air as they circle high above the farmland.

As the commotion persists, Tom's curiosity about the antagonists' whereabouts floods the little room left in his overburdened brain. Obsessed with the mystery of the songbirds' location, he looks up and glimpses the house.

Everything appears preserved in time. Little has changed—even the tiny wormholes embedded in the woodwork encapsulating the screened front door still lie in wait. As the sun shines onto the knotty lap siding, each snarled divot consumes the bright rays, turning the shine melancholy. It's as though the structure is intentionally sucking the life from its surroundings to balance the darkness hidden within its walls.

Its curious appearance escalates Tom's paranoia, and no matter how hard he tries to resist, his haunted past burrows into his mind. He has worked too hard to have timeworn wood be the one thing to divulge his history and ruin his extraordinary life.

He wants nothing more than to put the memory to rest, but his instability transports him to the night he finished what he knew must be done—his predatory acts to secure his future.

As he marches toward the front door, the birds sense a shift in his energy and squawk to warn the house of his oncoming approach.

Tom smirks, and his fascination takes over as he stares ahead at the home's picture window. Slowly, the whites of his eyes that surround his blackening irises are the only bright spot left in his being.

As darkness grips his heart, he remembers the night of their slaying like it was yesterday. His nostrils innately flare as if to catch a whiff of the iron scent stemming from their freshly spilled blood, and, met with euphoria, his eyes tightly shut.

The tip of his tongue caresses his lips to taste the smell.

Simultaneously, as Tom softly moans, a cloud mysteriously forms, shielding the sun. Everything appears calm as the shadowed sky reflects darkened thoughts on the land, and the scenery feels restored to the time when the murderous acts oc-curred.

As Tom nears the entrance, he can smell the hot cast-iron pot on the stovetop from outside, and his eyes spring open with excitement. Face-to-face with the screen door, his heart races. Everything from the incident seems so sharp to him.

Reaching for the door's handle, he glances at his trembling hand, causing his mind to replay that night. The calling chant of the wind enters through the tiny holes of the netted screen. Its melody is like a welcoming song that assures him everything will be okay.

As his fingertips touch the knob, the light from inside the kitchen illuminates the outline of his grandmother's body through the front window as she cooks dinner. The contrasting lighting of the scene is beautiful to him, almost like a work of art.

At that moment, she had no clue what was about to happen. She looks peaceful.

Wanting to see more, he opens the door and encounters the sound of plates clinking as they are placed on the dining room table. He quietly steps inside and shuts the door behind him. The thrill creates a trove of butterflies in his stomach, and it takes everything in him to control his giddiness.

"Is that you, Thomas?" his grandmother calls from the kitchen. "Come on. Dinner is ready, so hurry in now before it gets cold. I know how hun-gry you boys must be."

Knowing he must clean up for the jamboree, Tom looks toward the staircase, but he can't take his mind off his grandmother's voice. He turns toward the sound, wanting a better view, but the popcorn-textured makeshift wall divider obscures it. He takes a deep breath, tries to ground his drifting mind, and is met with the aroma of grits cooking.

His grandmother raises her voice from the other room. "You hear me, Tommy? I got everything all set and ready to go," she says.

Tom clears his throat. Not remembering the last time he had a home-cooked meal, his stomach growls as he runs his hands over his protruding ribs. Before deciding which direction to go, his feet develop a mind of their own, and he takes a giant step toward the kitchen.

Concerned he may be losing control, he squeezes his eyes shut and frantically shakes his head to clear his mind, trying to convince himself he is dreaming. "Now, come on, Tom, you know she isn't real. She's dead. They are both dead," he says.

Unfortunately, his attempt to escape the situation backfires. Rather than cleansing his mind, the barn's encounter fills the backs of his closed eyelids with movie-like images.

His grandmother's voice raises in pitch as she pleads, "Well, at least come in and sit for one bite. I went through all this trouble to cook your favorite grits for your birthday."

Her words cause Tom's eyes to spring open, and he fights the act, clenching his jaw and straining every muscle to keep them shut. His heart races. *It's all in your head, Tom. Just because they showed up in the barn doesn't mean they reside in the house. You own it; it's yours, not theirs. They died long ago.*

His thoughts build, and, keeping his eyes closed, he focuses on swiveling his body back toward the staircase.

The smell of hot cheesy grits fills the home like a morning fog taking hold of a meadow. Each whiff of air Tom draws in entices his grumbling stomach, and he tries to combat the savory smell's magnetic pull on his nostrils by taking shallow inhalations.

Lightheadedness creeps in with every hyperventilating breath, further skewing his ability to make rational judgments.

He tries to resume his mission to find a fresh change of clothes, but something keeps pulling him in a different direction. He hates the sensation of being meddled with, and it triggers a wave of rage. "You can't control me anymore. Do you hear me?" he shouts, wildly waving his arms thru the space in front of him. "I already killed you once! I-I'm not afraid to do it again. I won't let anything come between my pigs and me!"

His shouting starts a loud clunking noise that resonates deep within the wall's wooden structure. Tom flinches at the sound of the furnace kicking on. Little by little, the room's temperature grows hotter, causing excessive sweat to pool at his hairline.

He shifts his head toward the floor to divert the salty drips from reaching his eyes, but the mix of sweat, oil, and filth from his unwashed scalp still settles in the creases of his closed eyelids. The contaminated liquid seeps between his firmly shut skin folds, infiltrating his eyes and causing an unbearable stinging sensation.

Amid his suffering, his ears are accosted by additional loud clunking sounds within the walls. Overwhelmed by his frustration, he wants to make the culprit pay for his misery. He screams at the top of his lungs, "Get the hell out of my house!"

Each of his words projects droplets of spit onto the worn hardwood floor. He is familiar with how his anger escalates and holds his breath to roadblock its building nature. After a minute or so, intense pressure forms between his brows, and he loses control, turning his face beet-red. "Show yourself, you coward!" Tom yells with such fury that his lungs are depleted of air.

He draws in a prolonged wheezing inhale, then listens for the perpetrator to reveal themselves. Not hearing a response, he irrationally swings his arms in defense against what he cannot see. "You're not going to win. You wait. I'll show you!"

The clatter of the heating system abruptly ceases. Tom laughs at the turn of events. "Looks like someone knows what's best for them," he says.

The pain in his eyes is worse than before, and he realizes he must rinse them out to stop the suffering. Not wanting to resort to entering the kitchen, his mind fixates on the upstairs bathroom sink.

In a hurry, with his irritated eyes tightly closed, he makes his way toward the staircase. He stubs his toe but dismisses the collision as nothing more than a tiny annoyance compared to the agony of his eyes. He carries on, assuming the fixed item his digit encountered was the bottom step. He blindly waves both hands in front of him in search of the staircase's railing.

A shrieking whistle cuts through the musty air of the old farmhouse, and as it echoes through the home, it becomes clear that it's the sound of a teakettle climbing to a boil.

The eerie tune evokes the memory of scalding his hands under the bathroom sink faucet, and against his will, it thrusts him back into the violent night of his past. He cringes at the shrill sound as his heart's rapid pace makes him feel like he is fighting every minute to stop the recollection.

His temporary blindness makes every sound amplify his senses. The wailing pot shifts from low to high in tone, creating a profound paranoia in Tom that causes his muscles to stiffen and his heart to race. He fights the urge to scream as tingling stress hives erupt on his skin, turning his entire body splotchy shades of pinkish-red.

Tom knows what he must do: escape.

The whistling tea kettle's screeching matches the pent-up scream held captive in Tom's mind, and with each escalation in octave, so goes his anxiety.

Tom struggles to break free from the sound's psychological impact. His fingers connect with nothing but air as he fumbles for the railing, and, desperate; he realizes that the only option to find a grip is to open his eyes and look. He fears the pain that will ensue when the stagnant air touches his irritated pupils.

Regardless of the anticipated discomfort, he forces his lids apart.

His watering tear ducts cause his vision to blur and skew his view of his surroundings. It strangely filters everything, almost like he's ingested a hallucinogenic.

Still stuck on a repeating cycle, the whistling teapot's shrilling vibrato creates cracks in the kitchen cupboards' glassware. Every shattering echo adds to the intrusive song. The sounds fuel disarray in Tom's mind, and his brain spirals.

He tries to minimize the noise's impact by focusing on the pain in his eyes and toes. As he reigns in his attention, he works on gaining control and squints to help center his vision. But unfortunately, he catches something more than shapes and colors with his glare.

Something doesn't feel right to him. Without warning, his knees give out, and his body's downward momentum pulls him backward. His hands windmill behind him as he flounders to catch himself. To his surprise, his tailbone lands on the sturdiness of a thick wooden seat instead of the floor.

All at once, everything falls silent, including the whistling teapot. Tom's heartbeats grow louder, and his mind struggles to adjust even though the ambiance has shifted to a calmer tone.

Still suffering from blurry vision, he slowly reaches out to touch his surroundings, and his hands connect with a vertical row of thick wooden planks. His palms freeze against the oak.

Filled with a sinking feeling and hoping something will alleviate his suspicions, he glances down. A stain on his pants and the tiled floor beneath his boots catches his attention. His brief scan of the stain's details confirms that his vision has fully returned, and the sight triggers nausea to plague his stomach.

Working to calm himself, he inhales through his nostrils and gets a strong whiff of grits. Faint sounds of shuffling pans and footsteps moving across the floor surround him. Tom refuses to acknowledge their presence. "Shit," he says. He doesn't have to survey the room to confirm he has somehow found his way into the kitchen.

The sound of slopping food and the clink of a large metal spoon hitting the top of a porcelain plate radiates from the table. A cloud of steam rises from the fresh serving of grits in front of him, soothing his eyes with the moist heat.

Escaping the influx of warm mist, he raises his gaze and encounters his grandmother. The wooden legs of her dining room chair scratch against the floor as she pulls it across the tile to sit at the table.

Like in the barn, she appears normal, with no sign of injuries anywhere on her body. Each chunk of gray hair is wrapped perfectly around her pink foam curlers, and she is wearing the same green-patterned nightgown from the infamous night, with hand-knit slippers to match. The colors highlight the healthy glow of her cheeks, which are rose-tinted from working over the hot stovetop to prepare the meal.

Noticing Tom's stare, she makes eye contact, smiles, and motions to the plate in front of him. "I hope you are hungry. I made your favorite," she says.

Tom feels uneasy as he focuses on the plate of grits. His grandmother smiles and clears her throat. "Take a bite," she says.

The smell becomes stronger under his nose, and, unable to withstand the enticement, he forces his shaking hand to pick up his spoon. Before taking a mouthful, he looks at his grandmother. His unease makes her smile, and she chuckles to lighten the mood. "Don't worry. I'm sure it won't kill you," she says.

Something about her body language comes off as cynical, and, unsure of how to respond, he returns an awkward chuckle. Reluctantly, his trembling hand scoops up a spoonful of grits, and as he holds it to his lips, a bead of sweat rolls down his face. His grandmother's eyes widen as she watches the spoon enter his mouth.

While pretending to chew, Tom hides his concern about her intentions and waits until her eyes stray from his direction to spit it back onto his plate. He continues to analyze her actions, using his spoon to push the grits around on his dish to make it appear he is eating.

His grandmother takes in a vast mouthful of grits. As she enjoys the helping, the ends of her lips curl up, and she uses the empty spoon to point at the third plate she has set on the table. "Your grandfather must be working late tonight," she says.

Even though the reference makes Tom cringe, he realizes that, based on the timeline, she must not yet know what has happened to her husband. He stares at his plate to avoid eye contact and clears his throat. "What was that?" he asks.

With a loud gulp, his grandmother finishes her bite before speaking. "Well, I noticed your grandfather didn't come in with you, and he must be finishing up chores. He works so hard to keep up with the farm. I can't help but worry about him sometimes," she says.

Tom takes her impression that someone works harder than him as a low jab, which affects his self-worth. A wave of irritation festers in his chest, and he forces a cringe-worthy smile onto his face.

His grip tightens around his spoon, and he continues to push the food around his plate. "Yeah, you could say that, I guess," he says.

His grandmother notices the shift in Tom's voice and glances up to check on him. "Something wrong?" she asks.

Tom shrugs at first in response. Then, he blurts, "It's been a long day. You know, from working hard and stuff. It was pretty hot out there." Instantaneously, the sarcastic inflection of his voice causes the room to fall silent.

His grandmother shoves another helping of food in her mouth to fill the quiet and tries again to make conversation. "So, the big eighteen, huh? Have you thought about what you might do with your freedom?" she asks. "Maybe fly the coop?"

Tom's spoon freezes in the mound of food, and his jaw clenches tightly. Listening to his grandmother beat around the bush makes him angry, and he wants the conversation to end. He calmly cuts her off. "Grandpa already told me you both want me out of here." He laughs loudly. "So, you can cut the bullshit."

The hurtful words throw her off, and she falls quiet. Then, to avoid confrontation, she shoves another helping of food in her mouth and continues to chew.

Her lack of rebuttal makes Tom's blood boil, and his chest aches as he fights back his rage. He doesn't say a word, forcing her to sit in awkward silence. He believes being abrasive would only justify her desire to turn her back on him, and he refuses to give her the satisfaction.

His grandmother pretends to ignore him while shoving another helping of food into her mouth.

Tom stares at the table. As he fixates on her throat swallowing, his vision blurs. The egregious behavior of his grandmother ignoring him has chipped away at his mental state, pushing him to the end of his patience and setting him over the edge. With his spoon in hand, he slams a fist against the table to get her attention.

His grandmother loudly gasps, then jumps up from her seat. Picking up her plate, she rushes toward the sink and scrapes the rest of what's left of her dinner into an old coffee can fashioned into a compost bucket. The rhythm of her speech speeds up as she talks nervously over her shoulder. "We should wait for your grandfather to come in from the barn before we have this conversation," she says.

Her avoidance infuriates Tom and causes his grip around the spoon to squeeze so tightly that his hand cramps, and the handle bends. Easing his grasp, he drops the metal utensil onto the wooden table, and his eyes stare at a wall across the room.

Fixated in his thoughts, a smirk slowly forms on his face.

"He's dead," he says.

The demeanor of his delivery is so casual that the words seem to slip past his grandmother's ears at first. Then, while rinsing her dish in the sink for the third time, she finally responds to his statement. Her head perks up, and she nervously chuckles. "Don't be silly; he will be here shortly."

Tom can instantly feel the anxiety exuding from her body. The sensation of gaining the upper hand turns his grin into a sinister smile. He methodically pauses and shifts his gaze to the back of her head to gain a clearer view of her body language. "I killed him," he says, then sits silent, watching for her reaction.

Tom's shocking words cause tremors to appear in his grandmother's hands. The shaking becomes so fierce that she can no longer grasp her plate, and it tumbles from her fingers, shattering upon impact with the sink's basin.

The annoyance of the noise causes Tom's muscles to tense and his vision to darken. His mind drifts to the moment in the barn when his grandfather had told him he would be abandoned again. Fueled by the fresh wound, his anger takes over. "You think you can just get rid of me like one of the pigs?" he asks.

Fearful of her grandson's wrath and traumatized over the news of her husband's death, she refrains from turning around, frantically stumbling for words.

Tom's irritation is beyond reconciliation, and the sound of her scrambled vocabulary feeds the fire of his loathing. Playing off her fear, he springs to his feet and throws his chair across the room, further frightening her. He screams, "Answer me, you useless hag!"

Every consonant of his words projects spittle onto the back of her neck. Terrified of what he will do, she refuses to turn around and uses a dishrag to wipe the droplets from her skin.

Tom is livid over her lack of words, and he becomes submissive to his rage as he takes a stomping step closer to her. The weight of his foot causes the knife block next to the sink to rattle on the counter.

Trying to remain calm, his grandmother redirects her attention toward picking up shards of glass from the sink, but she can't seem to ignore the sound of the knives' sharp metal blades vibrating in the wooden block.

Tom becomes suspicious of her overly calm demeanor and believes she is calculating a plan.

Analyzing the movement of her shoulders, he notices a slight tilting of her head toward the knives. "I wouldn't do that if I were you," he says.

The idea of Tom knowing her plan of attack charges her adrenaline, and without pausing, she lunges to grab a weapon to defend herself.

Tom treats her attempt to fight for her life as a game, and, already one step ahead, he beats her to the punch. He grabs the cast-iron pot of grits from the trivet on the table with a single fluid motion and spins to face his grandmother just as she wraps her fingers around one of the knife handles.

He takes a second to watch her unsheathe it, then, with a loud grunt of fury, swings the pan with all his might, bludgeoning the back of her skull. The sound of her bones cracking echoes around the home's four walls.

She immediately becomes disoriented from the shock of the impact, gasping for air. She tries to cry for help, but nothing that exits her mouth makes sense. Her balance falters, she stumbles backward, and in the process, steps out of the heels of her hand-knitted slippers, which depart her feet as her body hits the floor.

The impact of the unforgiving tile on her bones forces her grip to release from the blade's handle, and it slides across the tile, stopping just out of reach of her weakened grasp. Even though Tom can see that her current state makes it impossible for her to fight back, he places the pot back on the table and fixates on where the knife has gone.

Spotting it, he seizes it from the floor and, in a blind rage, commits an unspeakable act of violence that leaves her torso slashed at least eighty times and him covered in the remnants of butchery.

Each puncture wound in his grandmother's flesh oozes a stream of crimson red that pools in different states of coagulation around her body. As the space can no longer contain the contents of the puddle, it escapes by forming small streams between the floor's grout lines.

The spectacle brings Tom pleasure as he licks a bloody speck from his bottom lip with a smile.

He enjoys the taste. "You should feel lucky. I think grandpa had it worse than you," he says, peering into her dilated pupils.

Becoming bored that the excitement is over, he releases his grip on the butcher knife protruding from her chest and notices the sound of water pouring into the sink. It reminds him of the moment she had thought she could outsmart him, and he chuckles.

A steam cloud fills the kitchen from the scalding water hitting the porcelain. The growing precipitation intrigues Tom, and taking a moment, he closes his eyes and deeply inhales the warm, moist air.

As he opens them to take another look at the carnage, nothing is what he expects, and he panics. Everything is different.

Tom is no longer in the kitchen; instead, he is standing in front of the sink's running water in the upstairs bathroom. The reflection staring back at him from the broken mirror's fogged glass causes him to release a guttural cry. "No, no, no!" he screams.

Looking down at the floor, he sees shards from the destroyed medicine cabinet and is sure he must be trapped in hell. Overtaken by his frustration, he closes his eyes and grips his hair with his fingers, trying to concentrate.

A loud creaking sound resonates from downstairs, quickly cutting through the white noise created by the running water.

The interruption makes Tom's heart race, and his eyes dart to the mess. "Fuck, it must be that woman from the barn. What's her name?" he says as his hands clench onto the edges of the porcelain bowl. "Claudia. Yeah, that's it. Claudia."

Trying to tame his internal worry about getting caught, he scans the room's surroundings, formulating a plan. The sound of footsteps makes him desperately spring into action, and he grabs the closest thing he can find to defend himself—the toilet plunger.

Claudia makes her way up the steps, following the sound of the running water to the closed bathroom door. She loudly knocks, concerned for his well-being.

The abrasive pounding makes him jump skittishly. As he hides the useless weapon behind his back, he clears his throat and tries to make his voice sound normal. "Yes? Who is it?" he asks.

Worried Tom may not hear her over the running water, Claudia presses her cheek against the door and yells back, "It's just me, Claudia. It seemed like you were taking a while, so I thought I should come inside to check on you and speed you along. I hope you don't mind! I know how important today is for you, and I am sure you don't wanna be late!"

Tom snaps himself out of his mood, and his brow furrows as he works to communicate normally, but the effort proves futile since he can't seem to get a word in edgewise.

Claudia giggles to herself and continues. "I mean, good thing I came in, or else you would have had one high water bill. You left the water in your kitchen sink running on high, but don't fret—I turned it off for you. As usual, Claudia comes to the rescue. You must have been hurrying, trying to make coffee or something, and you forgot about it. They always have some at the jamboree, and these cute 4-H girls sell it as a fundraiser. I think the proceeds typically go to a charity or something. I don't remember, but I know it's for a good cause," she says.

As Tom listens to her, the fast-paced rambling overwhelms him. Unable to track all the details, his grip loosens around the plunger's wooden handle, and he nervously clears his throat. "You sure do always think of everything."

Realizing he may sound smitten, he shakes his head over how stupid he must have come across. "How-how do you like the house?"

Claudia considers his trembling voice cute, and she smiles. "It's nice. Honestly, I'm surprised at how clean it is, with you being a bachelor and all. It's almost like no one even lives here," she says.

Her words ease Tom's anxiety, and, letting his guard down, he quietly tiptoes to return the plunger beside the toilet.

Caught up in her imagination, Claudia visualizes living in the farmhouse beside Tom and the precious life they would have together. She releases a dramatic attention-seeking sigh, then shifts her back against the door to get closer to him. "It may sound crazy, but I can see myself cooking a meal for you in your cute little kitchen. I can picture you coming inside after a long day caring for the pigs and sitting with me at the table. We'd make an awful cute family, you and I," she says.

Tom finds the idea of cohabitation with another human being unfathomable. The mere thought of seeing a person every morning is distressing. He closes his eyes, hoping the conversation will end.

Claudia suddenly realizes she may have pushed him too far and promptly switches the topic of conversation to distract him. "All right, now. I'll wait outside for you to load precious Olive in the car. We'd better get a move on. I will see you in two wiggles of a pig's tail!" she says with a giggle.

Tom opens his mouth to speak and stammers. "Okay-okay. I-I'll see you in a jiff," he says. Then, remaining still, he quietly listens through the sound of the running water for her footsteps to disappear.

The crash of the front door slamming echoes through the home. Tom breathes a sigh of relief and rushes to the sink to turn off the faucet. As he twists the handle, he notices the shards from the floor have disappeared. He glances up at his reflection in the mirror and is greeted by a perfect sheet of glass. The sight causes him to twitch nervously.

Not only is the mirror untainted, but so are his clothes. He is uncharacteristically dressed in a fresh red flannel shirt, dark-wash denim jeans,

brown cowboy boots, and his prized buckle attached to a belt made of black leather. Unable
to wrap his mind around the changing events, he
splashes water on his face to gain his bearings,
then waves his hands in circular motions to ensure
his movements match those of his reflection.

With a laugh, he shakes his head. "Boy, oh, boy,
Tom, you gotta get your imagination under control," he says.

Not wanting to be late, he rushes downstairs.
As he nears the front door, he takes a moment
to peer around the divider and into the kitchen.
Everything is spotless. He nervously chuckles and
shrugs. "I guess lack of sleep is like the hiccups. If
you don't shake it, you'll lose your mind," he says.

Flailing his limbs, he forces the last shudders to
depart his body. Then, whistling a happy tune, he
picks up his pace to the exit.

As he steps outside, he laughs at the ridiculous-
ness of his imagination. "You're a winner, Tom,
and don't you ever forget it," he says, then shuts
the door behind him. Standing on the porch, he
takes a deep whiff of the farm's smells while staring across the barnyard to investigate the commotion in the distance.

Claudia is where she said she would be, next to
her car, appearing frazzled. Tom squints to get a
clearer view. "What in God's name is she doing?"
he says to himself as he continues observing.

The passenger door of the convertible is wide
open, and the front seat is folded forward. Claudia

has taken it upon herself to load Olive in the car alone. She grunts as she tries to hoist the sow from her backside into the backseat of her car—Olive squeals with each shoving motion from Claudia's bony, well-manicured hands.

As Tom stares, admiring her valiant determination from a comfortable distance, the effort shown through her loud mutterings makes him chuckle.

Claudia gives Olive another forceful push and, shaking her head, smirks. Not in a million years would she have imagined herself being presented with such an extraordinary opportunity to catch a man.

Then, letting out another grunt, she pleads to the pig for help. "Come on, girl. You got to help me out a little. Your daddy will be here any minute, and it's our job to help ease his nerves and get you into this car," she says.

As Claudia shifts her body to put her shoulder into Olive's rear end, she notices Tom watching with a smile in the distance and, concerned about what part of the exchange he has observed, nervously smiles back.

Even though Tom can't hear exactly what she is saying, the shared moment between them makes him queasy. In response, his lips tense, and his cheeks quiver.

He cannot place the reason for his sudden change toward her, but he comes to terms with the fact that he views Claudia differently. She appears softer and less annoying. Each of her features is more appealing, almost making her somewhat attractive, and he can't help fantasizing about her involvement in helping take care of his family members. "There's just something about that woman. Maybe she isn't that bad after all," he says.

While carried away with his daydream of a potential future with Claudia, his eyes gravitate between his favorite women's faces next to each other.

With a last heave, Claudia releases a big groan, and the garish noise from the small woman startles Olive. The pig's front feet frantically paw at the leather backseat to solidify her footing, and as they gain traction, they unintentionally assist in hoisting her into the car.

It surprises Claudia that she has successfully loaded the pig herself, and as she watches Olive get comfortable, she takes a step back to revel in her impressive accomplishment. Suddenly, she realizes that the door is still open, and, not wanting to repeat the task, she lunges forward, flips the front seat to its upright position, and flings the heavy car door shut.

She notices a few dirt smudges on her skirt in the door's reflection and lets out a dramatic sigh after realizing Tom hasn't moved an inch. "Are you coming, or are you just enjoying the view?" she asks, playfully smirking.

Tom fidgets as his eyes focus on his cowboy boots. Then, knowing he must force himself out of his daydream, he gathers his words and gives an awkward wave. "Promise I'll be there faster than a racehorse," he says as he breaks into a sprint.

Claudia jumps into the driver's seat and promptly glances into her visor's mirror to check her makeup and hair while waiting for his arrival. "Men. Can't live with them, and sure as hell can't live without them," she says.

Chapter Seven

IF YOU AIN'T FIRST, YOU AIN'T SHIT

By the time Tom reaches the vehicle, Claudia has already made herself comfortable by turning on the ignition and changing the radio t's dial to her favorite bluegrass station.

As the first song nears the chorus, the car fills with the sound of a fiddle ramping into an improvisational riff. Each beat of the melody rolls through Claudia's swaying body, inspiring her to dance. She bops to the music as she prepares for the drive by securing the scarf on top of her head and pushing back her cat-eye glasses to the bridge of her nose.

Not wanting to appear too interested, she refrains from turning toward Tom and sneakily uses her peripheral vision to observe him taking his seat on the passenger side.

Adrenaline rushes through her veins, and she steps on the gas with a mischievous smile before he can entirely shut the door. The shift in the car's momentum swings the heavy door closed with a loud thud.

Tom flinches and nervously braces himself. Before this day, he's dwelled on every horrifying reason why he should not leave his property, especially the likelihood of panic attacks from venturing into unfamiliar scenery.

He attempts to relax by diverting his attention to Olive in the backseat. As the wind blows her face, each gust peels her lips apart, giving her the appearance of smiling. The passing air tickles her wiggling snout, and she sneezes. Her body shakes to ease the tingling, and her lush golden locks dance in the breeze.

A loud squeal of the car's tires causes Tom to turn back around and face the front abruptly as Claudia suddenly pulls the wheel to the right without either looking both ways or using a blinker. The car powerfully slides through the turn, kicking up gravel as it catches the road's shoulder before straightening back into her lane.

She enjoys the rush of living on the edge, but her erratic driving causes Tom to fearfully shut his eyes. Overwhelmed, he channels his oncoming anxiety by focusing on soothing thoughts, like cuddling with his pigs.

Claudia's body slides side to side with each wild steering wheel rotation. She spins the dial on the radio to crank up the volume and adds a bit of spice to the racket by hollering a loud "Suey!"

Even though the shrill scream sidelines Tom's attempt to meditate, it has the opposite effect that he would have expected. Instead of adding to his anxiety, her obnoxious behavior is so overwhelming that it makes him forget why he'd initially feared leaving his home.

Claudia glances at the passenger seat to see if he is enjoying his ride, and when she notices his eyes tightly closed, she sings at the top of her lungs to get him engaged.

The bumpy ride creates motion sickness that plagues Tom's stomach and turns his face green. Claudia tries not to fixate on his lack of response or let his despondent attitude taint her chipper nature. "Come on, now. I know you must know this song. It's not like you live under a rock or something," she says.

With a smirk, she glances at his stiff posture, then leans toward him and shoves his shoulder with a wink. Her complacency toward the road causes the car to swerve.

Thinking the jarring movement means they are about to crash, Tom's eyes spring open in a panic. Claudia ignores his flinching and interprets his opening eyes as a sign of his receptiveness. "See! I knew you would know this one!" she says.

Then, taking a moment of pause, she enthusiastically sings even louder with the melody. "Everyone is two-stepping these days... Even my mama dances the two-step, which says a lot."

As she chatters away, a wave of stomach acid travels up Tom's throat, and he fights it back down with a gulp. His lips quiver into a smile to hide his fear, and he nods, pretending to listen. "How much longer until we get there?" he asks.

His inquiry makes Claudia blush. "Are you tired of my company already?" she asks. Tom awkwardly laughs, not knowing how to respond.

Claudia promptly senses his rigidness. To alleviate the tension, she chuckles to lighten the mood. "I'm just messing with you," she says as she lifts her finger from the wheel and points ahead.

A small town rapidly approaches in the distance. To the left-hand side sits twenty acres of the dusty property designated for the fairgrounds. A dozen red barns surround a white picket-fenced patch of tilled dirt in the property's center—the competition arena. Livestock trailers of various sizes and colors sit in a line, with people gathered around each open back, unloading their hogs.

Tom takes a giant whiff of air. The familiar smell of cedar shavings and animal waste comforts him as his eyes lift to follow the direction of Claudia's pointing finger.

Olive loudly grunts and releases a squeal to let the world know she's on her way. Unable to contain her enthusiasm to just her vocal cords, she restlessly shifts her body, and her feet wildly scramble on the seat's leather upholstery. Sensing the pig's excitement match his, Tom gives her a toothy smile while reaching over the seat to pet her. "You smell that, Olive?" he asks.

In response, Olive wiggles her snout and curls her lips, mimicking his expression. He chuckles at how cute she is, and his voice raises an octave higher in excitement. "That's right, girl. It's the smell of victory," he says.

As the arched entrance approaches, the car slows down, and the blinker flickers to signal their turn. Unlike before, Claudia takes the corner more carefully to preserve her passengers' joyful moment.

With a slight rev of the engine and a gentle turn of the wheel, the tires tread across the cattle grid onto the uneven ground. As they bounce over the rough dirt road, Claudia breaks the silence by loudly announcing that they have arrived. "We're here!" She says. All three are in awe over the lively surroundings, like children entering a candy shop for the first time.

As she continues to drive past the row of pickups and pigs, Claudia appreciates the lively atmosphere as she focuses, like a hawk, on locating the perfect place to park. Scanning the passenger side, she notices Tom's open-mouth expression hasn't subsided. The term "poker face" is not a part of his vocabulary, and he can't hide being overwhelmed by the abundance of wandering pigs.

Claudia determines that a moment of privacy is essential before going inside and immediately recognizes what must be done. Her grip tightens on the leather steering wheel, and she cranks it to change the car's trajectory. As the convertible off-roads across the field to park a measurable distance away from the other competitors, the car's worn-out suspension and the addition of Olive's weight accentuate the impact of the bumpy, less traveled route.

They had never considered being the only convertible in the line of trucks, nor had they anticipated how they might stick out like a sore thumb. Flying under the radar is proving much more complex than expected.

Their engine steadily purrs as they slowly pass a man wearing a stained yellow t-shirt and straw cowboy hat. He stands idly, gossiping with a cliquish group of pig farmers next to one of the parked trailers. Mid-conversation, he glimpses the sun's reflection bouncing off the bright red paint of Claudia's car. The man rubs his eyes, sure that he is hallucinating, and upon realizing it is not his mind playing tricks on him, he frantically taps the others to rally their attention.

In unison, everyone follows his lead, checking out the spectacle he is referencing. They watch in disbelief as the out-of-place vehicle comically attempts to off-road. Unfortunately, the convertibles intrigue only lasts briefly before the group's leader points to what is displayed in the backseat.

Oblivious to anything other than what's ahead, Claudia continues her slow drive to the far end of the fair's designated parking area. She leans over the steering wheel to get a better view of the bumpy makeshift roadway in front of them. Unfortunately, she can only focus on trying to dodge as many potholes as possible to avoid bottoming out.

The music's tempo contradicts her intense concentration, and, cranked up to the maximum, it blares a looping honky-tonk chorus. Olive snorts in the backseat, joining in with the song's tambourine solo. Without a care in the world, she enjoys every moment of the relaxing ride.

She has been an indoor pig her entire life and is still getting used to the elements. Her teeth clack together as the breeze brushes against her skin. She attempts to eat the air each time it touches her face and shakes her head at the wispy currents as they comb through her wild mane. With each tousle of her hair, her teeth display a smile.

It's as though she knows she has an audience to entertain.

A short distance away, in the community of trailers, the word of Olive's golden hair is spreading like wildfire. Her fur quickly becomes the focal point of the event's conversation, and within minutes, all eyes migrate toward the pig in the convertible. Never having seen anything like it before, the attendees' mouths gape open as if entranced or petrified, like in the mythological tale of Medusa.

As she pulls into her selected parking spot, Claudia is oblivious to the buzz collecting at the fairgrounds. She turns off the car and sighs in relief that they have gotten there in one piece. "Here we are. This spot is perfect—nice and private," she says. A smirk falls over her face. Then, unbuckling her seatbelt, she switches off the radio and turns to face Tom.

Tom's nerves are overwhelming him. He can't help replaying the number of competition pigs he'd eyed on their slow drive into the grounds. At a complete loss for words, he silently faces forward, staring out the windshield as images of every pig they drove past play through in his mind, each with more detail than the last. *Short bristles, thin, fat, long snout, short snout, spots, no spots, clean, dirty.* Each element of the animals' uniqueness makes his thoughts run wild with comparisons.

The lack of verbal communication stirs Claudia's impatience to the surface, and she bites her tongue to stop herself from lashing out. Then, after taking a moment to cool down, she analyzes his stunned expression and reminds herself that, being that he generally keeps to himself, the crowds may be overwhelming him.

Suddenly, the loudspeaker kicks on, sending high-pitched static throughout the property and interrupting the gossiping whispers. It startles Tom, and he jumps in his seat.

Unfortunately, the sound also surprises Olive, and she becomes rambunctious, triggering her to flail and squeal in the backseat.

The unpleasant noise of the static overstays its welcome and agitates Claudia to the point of covering her ears. She glares toward the annoyance and spots the blurry outline of a man in the distance. He appears to be standing on a box, dressed in a cream-colored suit.

The figure's noticeably stout shape raises her suspicions regarding the perpetrator of the obnoxious racket's identity. She lowers her sunglasses to get a better view, and the sight of an extra-large brown cowboy hat on the man's head makes her eyes roll. "Good God. Of course, it's him. I swear, that man loves to hear himself blabber," she says. With a frustrated grunt, she pushes her cat-eyed rims up to shield her eyes and leans back in her seat.

The short-stature man with a big potbelly clutches his megaphone while standing in front of the crowd on a makeshift platform made of a wooden crate. His microphone releases an earsplitting squeal as he utters his first words, and he instantly ducks as if to hide. His hand, which showcases a collection of large, tacky high school sports rings, grasps the brim of his hat for dear life.

The man's comical movements draw attention to the big red barn behind him. The event's organizers have purposely left the doors at both ends of the building open to direct everyone's gaze to the beauty of the circular competition ring on the other side. The picturesque framing makes it clear that the architectural monstrosity has been designated as the entryway to the show ring.

The man carries on, ignoring the noticeable feedback from the speakers. The sleeves of his oversized suit bunch at his elbows as he waves his stubby arms in the air and points to a large sign made of burlap hanging from the edge of the roof. The freshly painted letters spell out a welcome message.

As he attempts to holler into the device again, the screeching does not subside. Stammering and embarrassed, his cheeks turn bright red, like the skin of a ripened tomato. Exercising his last resort, he pounds a fist on the device's mouthpiece. Rather than submitting to his dominant act, the microphone continues its persevering high-pitch whine with the addition of loud thuds from each brutal hit of his fist.

Claudia slouches further in her seat, hoping not to catch his attention, while her hands push harder against her ears to mute the unbearable racket.

After several minutes of torture, the harsh shrill finally snaps Tom from his paralyzed state, and in slow response, his head turns in the barn's direction. His new movement excites Olive. Thinking someone may finally end the ear-shattering noise, her feet bounce against the leather seat to encourage him.

Having been away from public interaction for several years, Tom feels confused by what he sees. "Do people here always act like that?" he asks. Not hearing an immediate response from Claudia, he peers at her and notices her hands covering her ears. "Claudia!" he says louder, waving a hand in front of her face.

Startled, Claudia instantly sits up with a loud gasp. "Jeepers," she says as her hand grasps her heart. "You can't scare people like that."

Tom points toward the barn. "Well, maybe you should listen better. I was trying to talk to you," he says with a sarcastic tone as his arm stiffly points. "Do people in this town always act like that?"

His demanding tone hits a nerve in Claudia. She doesn't like someone telling her what to do and refuses to stare in the direction of his pointing finger. "I don't know why they give him a microphone," she says with a dramatic huff. "Can you believe I went to high school with that dipshit? Well, I don't know what's worse: That I had to go to prom with him my senior year or that this town was stupid enough to vote him in as our mayor."

Tom becomes irritated by Claudia's lack of answer to the question and her overwhelming number of pointless details. Finally, overcome with frustration, he waves his hands in a crossing motion to cut off her rambling speech. "Stop it. I don't care about that!" he says.

Claudia's eyes grow wide, and she falls silent as she tries to process his abrupt anger. When Tom finally sees her lips no longer moving, he seizes the opportunity to speak.

In an attempt to get her to pay attention to his question, he becomes more animated, wildly flailing his arms toward the group gathered in front of the large red tin barns. "Woman, I am talking to you! Why are all of them staring?" he asks.

His aggressive behavior triggers Claudia's fight instinct, and, seeing his thrashing arms within inches of her face, she swats the air in front of her nose to defend herself. "Okay, okay, that's enough! Stop it!" she says as she rolls her eyes and looks toward the group's direction.

Tom is just pleased that she is finally listening.

The intent glare of the beady pupils' startles Claudia. Unlike many, who would be upset over the blatant breach of privacy, she is only flustered by not being better prepared to be at the center of attention. Had she known, she would have taken the extra effort to maintain her poise during their time parking.

She can't get past her more significant concerns to address the triviality of Tom's. "Huh..." she says. Tom ignores her odd reaction and glances at Olive, panting in the backseat.

Still wrapping her mind around the situation, Claudia replays every single body movement and facial expression she's made in the presence of the unexpected audience. She ducks behind the steering wheel and frantically primps her appearance. Once feeling rejuvenated, she straightens her posture and, with a coy smile, waves at a group of men flirtatiously. "That is quite the crowd," she says.

A few farmers bashfully blush, and one whistles a catcall at her. Feeding on the attention, Claudia blows a kiss to thank them for their compliments. "My, my, my," she says. It surprises her that she did not see the group of looky-loos earlier, and she brushes the oversight off with a giggle.

The mayor, impatient with the distraction, yells through the megaphone to calm the crowd. He is so animated in his attempt that he falls off the crate. "Let the pig jamboree begin!" he says. Rather than paying the mayor respect, everyone gathered at the trailers remains fixated on the sight of Olive in the back of the convertible.

Claudia lowers her cat-eyed sunglasses to the tip of her nose. "Well, that's odd. He is normally much longer winded than that," she says.

The mayor drops the megaphone and paces around the wooden crate to tame his frustration. Not receiving his deserved recognition, he kicks the dirt with his ostrich-skin cowboy boots while glaring at the onlookers.

Then, with a passive-aggressive smile, he sarcastically yells, "There must be something pretty good over there to take your focus away from your mayor. Especially one that has taken time away from his busy schedule to oversee the festivities of this fair competition."

Everyone ignores him as they talk about the pig's unusual fur.

Fed up, the man pushes his way through the crowd. As he snakes past the bystanders, he yells, "Excuse me, your mayor is coming through!" Even though no one is complying, he forges a pathway to the front. Overexertion causes sweat to drip from his chin, and he pulls on the lapel of his suit jacket to allow airflow to his chest. "What in God's name is so fascinating?"

He plants his feet and furrows his brow, focusing on the distant car. Something brushes against his shoulder, and, breaking his gaze, he catches sight of the culprit—a man with dirty pig shit-stained overalls.

The bystander quickly realizes the identity of the man he has bumped into and fumbles to speak. Never having seen a celebrity before, he nervously wipes his hands against his tainted pants to clean them, then extends one out for the mayor to shake. "Jeez, Louise, where are my manners? My name's Mud. That's what they call me around here," he says. His attention shifts to the parked convertible in the distance. "That pig out there, Mr. Mayor—you see it? I swear, it's covered in gold. Its hair's so nice; I would put it on my woman's head."

His raving words intrigue the mayor. Wanting to be apprised of the situation, he squints harder toward the convertible to get a better view. "Is that so?" he asks. Still trying to decipher what he's talking about, his nearsighted vision makes everything appear slightly fuzzy.

Attempting to stall, he lets out a sarcastic laugh. "Well, I hate to break it to you, but pigs don't have hair, so I would be mighty curious to see what your woman looks like if pig bristles on her head would be an improvement."

The sound of his rumbling laughter shifts Mud's demeanor. Clearing his throat, he sarcastically cackles along with the mayor, digging his boots into the dirt. "You know, I'm not sure I follow what you're getting at," he says. He shifts his weight and pushes up his sleeves as if ready to fight.

The sound of his knuckles cracking alerts the mayor, and his expression goes stale. Worried about getting hit, he takes a step forward from the crowd. "I'm sure it's just one big misunderstanding," he says with a much subtler demeanor.

Simultaneously, Claudia turns toward Tom. Lightly placing her hand on his knee, she shakes it with excitement. "You see that, honey? I think they are staring at that little star sitting back there," she says, pointing her thumb over her shoulder at Olive. "She is getting treated just like the princess she is."

As Tom intently listens to Claudia's pep talk, her words wrap a blanket of warmth around his heart, and amid his rushing emotion, he turns to the backseat to stare at his most prized possession. His favorite pig is absolute perfection in his eyes.

Olive wiggles her snout to cool herself down from the heat. A gust of wind infiltrates her nostrils, and her head shakes as she lets out a loud sneeze. The motion showcases her long, curly blond locks, and her lush mane dancing through the air makes her look like a model in a shampoo commercial.

Tom is beside himself as he stares at her infinite beauty. His eyelids widen with wonder, and his smile stretches from ear to ear at the sight. "She sure is something special," he says.

Claudia is smitten with how much he cares for Olive and wishes a partner would treat her with the same love and affection. As she fixates on how much Tom loves his dear pig, she fantasizes about her future with him. "Yup, you sure are," she says as her cheeks turn pink upon realizing her impetuous answer. Then, clearing her throat to cover the slip-up, she nervously giggles. "I mean... *she* sure is. You did a fine job with her."

Tom leans over the seat to scratch Olive's ears, noticing neither Claudia's infatuation nor her snafu.

The mayor's vision shifts to the driver's seat as he stares across the dirt parking lot and smirks. "By God! Well, speak of the devil," he says. Then, thinking he recognizes Claudia's face, his weight shifts back and forth in his boots as he contains his excitement.

Not wanting to embarrass himself by acknowledging someone he mistakenly thought to be someone else, he focuses harder on her profile to confirm his suspicion. His mind falls into tunnel vision, and he tunes out everything surrounding him.

Slowly, the sound of the crowd gets lower, and everyone's mood takes a drastic turn, morphing from high-level enthusiasm to low-grade rumbles of defeat. Then, with a few last complaining whispers, the crowd disperses toward the barn behind them.

After hearing a commotion shift, Claudia lowers her sunglasses to see what's happening. Her change in position gives the mayor the validation he needs, and his eyes open with disbelief. "I knew it was her. The one that got away," he says as he shakes his head. "Momma said she'd come back around one day, and I guess that day is here in the present. After this, I'll question nothing my momma says again."

He glances at the sky. "I swear to God; I will be a better man." Unable to hold himself back any longer, he takes a deep breath to prepare to yell to her, but the sounds of trucks hooking onto their trailers startle him, derailing his mission.

As miscellaneous pigs squeal, a man shouts over the commotion. "Hey, mayor! We are leaving!"

Confused by the events, the mayor briefly ignores the disgruntled farmer to glance back at the convertible. He sees that Tom has climbed over the seat to sit in the back with Olive while Claudia remains alone in the front, stationed behind the steering wheel.

The mayor knows he must fulfill his political obligations since the pig jamboree is a big money earner for the city council. Figuring he has a few minutes to spare before Claudia takes off, he reluctantly turns around to try de-escalating the situation. His eyes dart to the farmer who had yelled at him, and he realizes the man is someone he knew from childhood. "Tanner, wait!" he shouts.

Tanner pissed off with the day, has already loaded his competition pig into the trailer. His dirty light-washed jeans and old white undershirt reflect the blood, sweat, and tears he has put into his preparation for the jamboree. Blatantly ignoring the mayor, he keeps his head down. His jaw tightens, cheeks fill with air, and his lips purse as he spits a wad of dip to the ground and flings open the door of his rusted truck.

While hustling forward to catch him, the mayor frantically scans the fairgrounds to see what everyone else is doing. The remaining farmers have finished collecting their competition pigs from the barn. Squeals ring from each snout as, one by one, they prod the animals back into their respective transportation.

The scene is absolute chaos.

The mayor picks up his pace to get to Tanner, knowing that he will have the lowdown on what has occurred. Concerned he didn't hear him calling the first time, he alters his approach, waving his hands and yelling, trying to get his attention.

"Tanner, come on, pal, where are you going? I am sure we can figure this out!" he says.

The mayor's voice aggravates Tanner, and, refusing to make eye contact, he hops inside the silver pickup cab and slams the door shut.

Then, without hesitation, he starts the car and revs the engine. His pig squeals from the trailer, and he turns on his radio to drown out the surrounding noise.

Running out of options, the mayor continues to shout, "Wait!" His boots slide through the dirt as he tries to halt his momentum in front of the truck's driver-side. The mayor taps on the window, but the heavy metal music pouring from the cab only becomes louder. The car's wheels move, and, worried about his toes getting run over, he dramatically jumps out of the way.

Tanner chuckles as he catches the scene from the corner of his eye. "Boy, don't you be asking for my vote next election," he says.

The mayor is stunned by the man's lack of friendliness, and, while removing his cowboy hat to wipe away profuse sweat, he watches him leave, his truck and trailer bouncing over potholes all the way to the fairgrounds' exit.

Almost in unison, the other trucks' engines start, and they begin to exit the grounds. One by one, he watches his city council budget drive away, and, desperate to save at least enough for the office coffee, he spins around to see who remains.

Mud is a bit behind the rest, leisurely latching up his trailer. With a hat in hand, the mayor waves it back and forth over his head to get his attention. "Hey, you there!" he says.

Mud completes what he is doing, hears the shouting, and turns to look. The sight of the mayor curtails his cheerful demeanor. He remembers the rude words exchanged earlier and has no interest in an insult-filled repeat.

The brief eye contact is enough for the mayor to use as an invitation to proceed, and, having no other options, he runs in the farmer's direction. "You know, I was only joking earlier. I didn't mean none of that stuff I said," he says.

As the mayor approaches the rusty blue truck, Mud tries to ignore him, but he loves to gab and is a sucker for apologies. He stops next to the driver's side door and contemplates the mayor's frazzled state. "That was a real low blow, but you're lucky I'm a Godfearing man, so I guess I can forgive you this once," he says.

The mayor feels relieved. Placing his hat back on his head, he holds up a hand to thank him and, struggling to catch his breath, continues asking his question. "Why in the world did everyone leave?" he asks.

While scratching his head, Mud stares off in the distance at the last trailer exiting the grounds. "It's plain as day: they believe this year's jamboree is rigged," he says.

His answer confuses the mayor. "'Rigged?' What do you mean by 'rigged?'"

Mud shifts his focus to the red convertible across the field. "They said that you allowed a cheater to compete in the competition. You said it yourself—pigs don't have hair, but that one over there has a mighty fine coat," he says.

The mayor pauses for a moment to formulate a politically favorable response. "Well, you can tell everyone that, as mayor, I'll take care of anyone trying to mess with our town," he says. Then, clearing his throat, he puffs out his chest. "As the mayor of his town, I'll find out if they are cheaters and make them pay. That's the law."

Mud opens his car door and turns to give the mayor one last word of advice. "I know that the election is coming up real soon, so you better try to fix this lickety-split, or you'll need to find yourself a new office," he says.

Utterly pleased with his input, Mud hops inside his truck and starts the engine. As he slowly drives toward the exit, he watches the mayor making his way across the field in his rearview mirror and laughs. "You show them who's boss."

Over halfway across the dirt path, the mayor waves toward Mud's truck as it gets smaller in the distance.

Meanwhile, Tom and Claudia fixate on the fairground's designated exit. They have witnessed every vehicle vacate the premises and are trying to wrap their heads around why everyone has fled.

Upon realizing that every competitor is gone, Tom cuddles closer to Olive and tightens his arms around her in a giant hug. "Does that mean we're the winners?" he asks.

Not knowing how to respond, Claudia stumbles for her words, and taking one last peek at the barn, she notices the mayor darting toward them. Swiftly putting on a poker face, she pushes up her sunglasses as if to disguise herself and calmly starts the car's engine. "Well, it seems like we'll soon find out," she says.

She avoids looking at the man approaching, keeping her gaze directed at the windshield. Her knuckles turn a shade of white as her hands clutch the steering wheel.

The engine's roar snaps Tom to attention, and as his head turns, he is met with the mayor's beet-red face staring back at him.

Working to catch his breath, the mayor tries to clear his winded lungs with a loud heave. Tom doesn't care about the purpose of the noise; he finds the raspy tone unbearable.

Even though the man's presence is severely off-putting, he fights his uncomfortable feelings; his yearning to know how they placed in the competition far outweighs any deterring qualities. Tom painfully gives an enthusiastic smile to break the ice. "Did we win?" he asks.

As the mayor's lungs release a wheeze, he gazes at Tom sitting in the backseat and immediately finds himself thrown off-guard. During his pep talk earlier, Mud referenced the man as a stranger or outsider, but he was not. He recognizes his face.

Taking a step back, he places his hands on his hips and takes a few slow breaths to finish calming his pulsating heart from his infrequent cardio. "Wait a moment. I know who you are," he says as he points to Tom.

The gesturing motion of his finger, paired with Tom's lack of knowing him, adds to his discomfort. Finally, after inappropriately laughing at Tom's guilty expression, the mayor continues, "You're that boy that was in the foster system with the dead mother," he says.

Each word digs at Tom's soul, causing him to melt in his seat.

As the mayor watches him squirm, he knows he has guessed correctly. Being a politician, he prides himself on remembering the most obscure faces and treats the situation like he has won a trivia session. With a squealing shout, he throws his hands into the air and slaps his knees upon their descent. "Woo-wee, I just knew it! Boy, oh, boy, am I good, or am I good? I was taking a stab in the dark, but I thought I recognized that face, and boy, was I right," he says.

Continuing to laugh obnoxiously, he places his hands on the car door and tilts his upper body inside. As he leans over to get a better look at Tom, he becomes distracted by the pig's hair and, mesmerized, tries to touch it. "Wow, its hair is so unusual."

Olive's eyes lock on the motion of the mayor's hand, and, noticing the extra meat on his bones, she thinks he's a snack. Her teeth rapidly clack at his wiggling digits, but she only gets a taste of air.

With a delayed reaction, the mayor jerks his fingers back and hides his hand inside his suit jacket. Never having lived on a farm or had something try to bite him before, the sow's behavior appalls him. "You got to muzzle that thing," he says.

His statement offends Tom, and he lightly places his hand on Olive's back to comfort her. He grits his teeth to fight back his anger. "What did you say?" he asks.

The mayor notices a unique intensity emulating from his eyes that he hasn't seen before and, not wanting to pick another fight for the day, backs off. "Woah, there, partner. I was just a little shocked, that's all. I'm sure that thing is friendly as a kitten," he says.

Unable to take much more, Claudia's fingernails dig into the steering wheel. Finally, she is at the end of her patience and gives up on holding back. Her once-docile personality snaps. "Jesus Christ, Milburn, answer the question already. Did he win or not?" she says.

Hearing his God-given name makes the mayor cringe, and, giving a sarcastic smile, he shifts his attention to the driver's seat. "I thought that was you," he says as he taps the top of her head. "I think the last time we talked was—"

His drawn-out way of flirting makes her angry, and before he can finish the sentence, she spins around in her seat to cut him off. "Senior prom. We all know. The whole *town* knows. That's what happens when everyone's inbred. You ditched me for Marla," she says.

The mayor winks at her. "I see you are the same little spitfire I fell in love with back in high school," he says.

Trying not to gag, Claudia rolls her eyes and redirects him. "Did he win or not?" she asks.

Even though he knows Tom and Olive have won, the mayor shrugs. "Why do you care? Would you like him to win?" he asks. Then, sure she's playing hard to get, he leans toward her to whisper, "You know, being mayor, I have some special privileges. I can always pull a few favors."

Tom, sitting quietly in the backseat, finds the interaction comical. Uncomfortable, Claudia leans away with disgust. "You know his pig is not like any other around. It deserves to win just based on its fantastic hair alone," she says.

Her hostility irritates the mayor, and he pulls back to make it appear mutual. "Lighten up, woman. It would help if you learned how to take a joke. And yes, he won. The whole competition packed up and left when they saw this pig. Everyone's making accusations it's cheating," he says as he gawps at Olive.

Ignoring the latter half of his words, Tom smiles from ear to ear. "What did we win?" he asks. Claudia wants to share the moment of happiness. With a huge grin, she turns to face the backseat.

Immediately, the mayor pauses. Claudia's friendly reaction toward Tom sparks his jealousy. In addition, he finds it strange that Tom doesn't give a second thought to people questioning his character.

Regardless of his suspicions, he knows he still must fulfill his political duty. So putting his unease aside, he clears his throat to give his usual rehearsed prize speech. "Let's see what our winner gets to take home today. The champion of this competition will leave here with a six-month supply of feed delivered from our local grain store, and wait—that's not all. He will also take home two—yes, two—hundred bucks in cold hard cash," he says.

Reaching into his pocket, he pulls out a wad of bills and begins tossing them in Tom's direction as if making it rain on him.

Overjoyed, Tom swats at the money, trying to catch it.

As the mayor watches the paper fall to Tom's lap, he catches a glimpse of his belt buckle, which looks oddly familiar. "Say, that's a mighty fine belt buckle you have there. The last time I saw anything similar, it was worn by a dear friend of mine who disappeared not too long ago," he says.

Tom continues collecting his money, but the mayor's words trigger something in Claudia. "Danny Boy went missing?" she asks.

Seeing how the news affects her, the mayor nods and walks to the opposite side of the car to get a closer look at Tom's buckle. "The resemblance is so uncanny," he says, reaching toward it while reading the writing. "Slightly different, however. He had D.B. engraved on his, with a different pig."

Tom swats at him to get away. "Don't touch that. You'll smudge it," he says.

The grown man's reaction is off-putting to the mayor, and he quickly withdraws his hand. "All right, all right," he says, then puts his hands in his pocket.

Realizing what is going on, Claudia begins to become disgruntled. "If I didn't know better, I'd think you're accusing him of something," she says.

The mayor shrugs. "I mean, you should care just as much as me about the situation," he says. Irritated by her taking sides, he continues. "Who is this hick to you, anyway? Look at him."

Angered by his disrespect, Claudia feels a wave of rage taking over. Thinking of what will hurt Milburn the most, she blurts out a comeback. "He's my boyfriend. We're in love," she says smugly.

The mayor rolls with laughter to cover up his fuming anger. "This guy is your new fellow? That's a laugh," he says. Taking a moment, he studies Tom's face to see his response. "Is that your girlfriend? Just look at yourself. You think you're going to keep her attention?"

Olive reads the negative energy he is exuding and squeals. To protect Olive, Tom twists the handful of bills to control himself from snapping. "Stop it. You are offending the lady," he says.

His words make Claudia feel he cares, and she grins. Without hesitation, she eggs him on to continue. "You tell him, sugar," she says.

Even though her statement throws him off, Tom has no time to think and must defend his pig. "We're getting married," he says. Claudia gasps.

The mayor is beside himself over the announcement, and he eyeballs Claudia for validation. "Is that true?" he asks.

A mischievous grin comes over Claudia's lips, and she shrugs. "You heard the man," she says. Then, feeling a rush of adrenaline, she spins around in her seat and, taking the car out of neutral, steps on the gas.

As the engine revs, the peeling tires kick dirt up in the mayor's face. Claudia delights in seeing his dumbfounded expression in the rearview mirror and laughs. For the first time in her life, she feels she has the upper hand in her future. Entering married life, she will finally prove everyone wrong and escape the small-town mentality; she will make something of herself.

As the mayor's face becomes smaller in the distance, she can taste her new beginning with Tom and finds the prospect exhilarating. Feeling invincible, her foot rests heavily on the gas pedal. Every jarring bump caused by her reckless driving over the uneven potholes makes her smile. She loves the thrill. "That was exhilarating!" she says.

With a sigh, she feels herself slip into a daydream. "Imagine me becoming a Mrs.? It's a moment I've only dreamed of and is finally coming true."

Tom cannot hear a single word over the engine's roar and obliviously smiles while focusing on Olive's jowls flapping in the wind.

Chapter Eight

TILL WHOSE DEATH DO US PART?

The newly proclaimed lovebirds display their happiness in silence for the remaining car ride home.

Still elated over the recent win, Tom assumes Claudia feels the same and that her unusually peachy demeanor is due to their winning the jamboree.

On the other hand, Claudia is convinced Tom's jubilance only has to do with his being smitten with her and his newly discovered puppy-dog love.

Although both are wrong about the reasons for their partner's gleaming grins, the car's euphoric energy is preserved because Claudia and Tom are happy keeping to themselves and reveling in their interpretations.

Lucky for Tom, his surprising marriage proclamation has placed Claudia in a quiet pandemonium state. The entire ride home, she is dead silent, consumed with mental deliberation about every detail regarding their impending nuptials.

Claudia floors it down the driveway of the little farmhouse and slides to a stop in front of the barn. After taking a deep inhalation of her future, she hops out of the car and flips the driver's seat forward.

Seeing her chance to escape, Olive scrambles past the seat and runs toward the barn. Tom jumps out of the convertible and sprints after her like a piglet chasing its mother. "I know you're excited to tell the others, but you best not let this winning get to your head," he says.

Olive impatiently stands outside the barn's entrance, squealing to be let inside with her friends.

Claudia flips the driver's seat back and looks at Tom, who is already at the barn opening the door. "You have a date in mind?" she asks.

Mid-heave of the heavy sliding door, Tom lets out a loud grunt. As it rolls open, he brushes the dirt from his hands and chuckles at Olive darting inside. Feeling like someone's staring at him, he glances back to the car and notices Claudia's crossed arms and tapping foot. "What was that?" he asks.

"Our ceremony—do you have a date in mind? There's planning stuff I gotta take care of, like decorations," Claudia says.

Tom scratches his head in confusion. "'Our ceremony?'" he asks.

Claudia's eyes instantaneously roll. "This isn't the time to be cute and play games, Tom. I'm being serious. It's only a matter of time before the whole town hears the news from that blabbermouth mayor, so I need to get a move on and make plans for this shindig," she says.

As Tom listens to her ranting, he begins connecting the dots from the earlier conversation with the mayor and, seeing how things could have been misconstrued, chuckles. "Well—" he says.

Before he can get another word out, Claudia cuts him off. "You know what?" she says, flagging him to remain quiet. Tom tries to speak again, and she hushes him. "Never mind. Don't worry your little self over the details; I'll take care of it," she says.

With a quick pivot of her body, she races toward her car, climbs inside, and slams the door shut. She reaches for the keys and turns the ignition. "Figure out what you wanna wear, and I'll be back after I talk to some local places about the frilly stuff."

Tom notices a small break in her speech as she checks her reflection in the visor mirror, and he tries to seize the opportunity to speak, but not much comes out. "But..." he says.

Claudia steps on the gas pedal, revving the car's engine. "Toodle-doo!" she says. She shifts the car into drive and floors it, leaving a cloud of dust and rocks behind the red convertible as she speeds down the driveway.

The nature of her abrupt departure confuses Tom. He can't determine how things have been left; nothing about the conversation seemed settled. As he watches the car fishtail down the road, he closes his mouth to keep from swallowing the dirty cloud.

Realizing he can no longer spot the vehicle in the distance, a wave of panic sets in, and his heart races. As each palpitation grows more robust, he rushes into the barn to seek comfort.

Olive is patiently waiting by the pen's gate to be let back in with the herd, and upon making eye contact with Tom, she squeals. The wrinkling of her snout makes him smile. Worried that his distraction has kept her waiting, he sprints to unchain the door and let her in. "I'm sorry, girl. I didn't mean to leave you standing here," he says.

Olive fixates on the chains loosening around the entry, and her nose nudges the opening, creating a space wide enough to squeeze through. The rest of the herd observes the commotion and swarms to greet her. Olive shows her joy at their gathering with soft oinks and nuzzles.

Tom follows her into the pen's confinement and secures the door. As he watches the reunion, the sound of their snorting exchanges puts a smile on his face, but his enjoyment is short-lived as he remembers what Claudia had said about their betrothal. A wave of anxiety returns, similar to before, but much worse. This time, fear overtakes his mind.

Excited to see one another, the pigs playfully chase each other around the pen while their loud snorts echo between the barn's tin walls. Not wanting to spoil their merriment, Tom presses his back against the gate to stabilize his trembling knees and keeps quietly to himself.

Using the sturdy metal, he slides down and sits on the edge of the concrete slab. Then, in an attempt to gain control of his shallow breathing and rapid heartbeat, he leans over his knees and places his head in his hands to refocus his thoughts.

The sensation of something brushing up against his leg breaks his concentration. It's Olive. With each slight tilt of her body, she attempts to console him. The familiarity of her leaning weight eases Tom's building nerves. Refraining from looking up, he extends a hand to pet her between her ears, and as each tip of his finger brushes a single strand, he finds solace in the texture of her fur.

He knows he must tell her of his new engagement, but the last thing he wants to do is upset his favorite pig. As he sits in his silence, he swallows a gulp of air, causing tension to roll down his throat and into his chest. Finally, never having been able to harbor secrets from her, he blurts everything out. "I'm afraid there is something I have to tell you."

A round of snorting resounds from Olive's nose, and the rapidity of her response worries Tom. Knowing he must face her, he hesitantly turns to peer into her eyes.

With a deep inhalation, he sighs, then spills his guts. "It's not easy to tell you this, but I'm unsure what to do. Remember when that unpleasant man came to the car at the jamboree to tell us that we won?" he asks.

Distracted by a peculiar smell near her feet, Olive pushes her nose into the dirt to investigate what it is. Thinking she is upset over the conversation, Tom changes his explanation to a request for forgiveness. "It's nothing... I'm sorry. I swear, I can take care of it. I never pictured myself as the marrying type, anyway," he says.

He shakes his head to clear his conscience, and noticing Olive's snout still pressed against the dirt, he continues, "I mean, you, yes, but her, no."

Swiftly, he plunges to his knees to make eye contact with her. The jarring movement of his body catches Olive off-guard, and, not seeing him for anything other than another animal lunging toward her, she instinctually jumps. Tom, groveling, crawls in her direction. "Please, please forgive me," he says.

Suddenly, she recognizes him as the man who feeds her. She charges at him and, with a single headbutt, lets out a playful squeal.

As Tom listens to the tone of her voice, his whole body freezes. He has always understood the general context of her wants. Having been the one to raise her, he takes pride in interpreting her desires, like an infant's crying, but something is different—now, he seems to understand every syllable of her speech. Lifting his chin to watch her moving mouth, his eyes widen. "You...you can talk?" he asks.

Overcome with hunger; Olive lunges at him again. This time, her nose nudges the tops of his hands, and her squeal grows louder.

Tom's face exudes confusion as he listens closely to every cry. Then, suddenly, without cause, he springs upright on his knees. "Wait, let me get this straight. You are saying you think I should marry her?" he asks.

The abruptness of his upward movement excites Olive, and, wanting to hurry him along to fetch her food, she hops up and down on her front feet.

Still uncertain of her answer, Tom, flustered and lightheaded, grabs onto the fence's metal links to pull himself to his feet and, to calm his anxiety, walks the perimeter of the pen.

Olive sits her back half on the dirt and quietly oinks while her focus shifts from food to watching him pace and listening to his mumbling thoughts.

As Tom converses with himself, he takes another lap around the dirt floor, and an epiphany pops into his head. Shaking the jitters from his shoulders, he turns to face the gate and chuckles. "I never thought of it like that," he says.

The idea's brilliance causes him to throw his hands into the air, and he laughs. Then, digging the heels of his boots into the dirt, he spins around and points at Olive. "You know what? You, girl, have both beauty and brains."

The edges of his lips crack into a smile that extends from ear to ear. "I'm not playing around when I tell you: you're one rare package."

Olive doesn't care about a single word coming from his mouth. Her only fixation is on his lack of movement toward the grain bin, and the delay makes her impatient; she's hungry. As her frustration builds, the squealing noises that leave the back of her throat morph into shrieking.

The brashness of her cry centers Tom back to reality, and, knowing he has many details to sort out, he darts toward the gate to get to work. "Why didn't I think of that?" he asks. Then, placing a hand on the latch, he shakes his head. "If I marry her, and no one ever catches onto us, it will be our little secret... a love story for the ages."

He gives a boisterous laugh and smiles while staring off into the distance. "Brilliant."

His ranting makes Olive lose patience. She can no longer take her grumbling stomach. Desperately wanting to get his attention, she charges the back of his knees, but her forehead overshoots the target, colliding with Tom's rear end.

Tom's face turns bright red, and with a playful jump, he grabs his backside. "Woah, now, girl," he says. Then, turning to glance at her, he winks. "If we're going to make this work, no one can know how we feel about each other."

Dwelling on the fact that he is still not moving toward the grain bin causes Olive's stomach to ache even more. She squeals again at the top of her lungs, trying to get his attention.

Tom surmises that her cries are due to her mourning the loss of their undeniable love, and, unable to take seeing her upset, he somberly turns around to finish unlatching the gate. "I know, I know, this may be hard," he says as he lets himself out.

Shutting the door behind him, he glances at her one last time. "No matter how it may appear, remember—my heart only beats for you. Nothing will ever come between us. Cross my heart and hope to die. I promise."

As Olive watches him break into a smile, her squealing pleas become frantic. She wants food. Recognizing the hunger pains in her cry, the other pigs join in. They, too, want to get their daily share of grain.

The shrill noise resonating through the barn overwhelms Tom's mind, filling him with unbearable anxiety. Finally, unable to stand it any longer, he turns around to leave. "I know, I know. I'm going," he says as he heads toward the door.

Halfway across the barn, he sees the fifty-gallon steel drum of grain. The sight of the lid tightly sealed on top causes him to remember that it hasn't been opened for at least a day. He rushes toward it in a panic. The pigs know what comes out of the can, and they squeal with excitement upon seeing him approach it.

Tom is consumed by guilt over his neglect. "You must think I'm awful," he says. Removing the lid, he spots the makeshift scoop fashioned from an old tin coffee can buried underneath a layer of pellets. He grabs it and scoops up a large helping of food. "Why didn't you guys tell me I missed your feeding today? Huh? You want me to look bad?"

Babbling to himself, he spins around with the overflowing can in his hands. His jerking momentum causes the grain to tumble over the sides and scatter across the concrete. The pigs, paying no mind to his neurotic conversation, continue to squeal frantically.

Immediately, Tom fears he may have come across as hostile, and with a deep breath, he corrects his demeanor. "My nerves must have gotten the best of me. That pig jamboree this morning was just one big heap of stress. I hope you will forgive me. You know how I get when my schedule is off-kilter," he says with an anxious chuckle.

Then, not paying any attention to the mess he's created, he stumbles to the edge of the fence.

Glancing at Olive's lush fur, a spark of excitement reflects in his eye. "We won, though... Did she tell you that?"

Like tossing breadcrumbs to a flock of birds, he chucks the contents of the tin can across the dirt floor of the pigpen. Small brown pellets rain across the backs of the hungry animals, and the pigs bite at one another as they frantically swarm the food.

Tom watches the feeding frenzy apprehensively and chuckles nervously. Then, worried the herd may hold a grudge, he continues to stammer for words that will return him to their good graces. "Thanks to that little gal over there, there will be plenty more where that came from. She won us a whole heap of food," he says.

As he watches the wave of contentment brought on by the meal, he wants nothing more than to keep the pigs happy. Even though they have yet to receive their prize winnings, he gives them more pellets than usual in anticipation of their windfall.

He rushes back to the barrel, scoops another can of grain, and tosses it into the pen. "You'll never be hungry again!" he shouts. He stands proudly, looking at the herd, and revels at how his abundance makes them glimmer.

Each of them snorts as they dig their snouts into the dirt, rummaging for pellets. While they continue their search, Tom proactively runs to get more grain and, upon his return, tosses it over the fence.

As their stomachs fill and their ravenous behavior subsides, Tom recalls how Claudia used a technique to shift the mayor's thoughts in her favor. Still concerned over the pigs' irritation at him due to his lax oversight, he utilizes what most would consider a manipulative approach—deferring blame by garnering sympathy.

He slowly tilts his chin and eyes toward the ground. "You think you can forgive me?" he asks. As he clutches the empty can in his hands, he refrains from lifting his head, waiting for an answer.

Rather than the response he was fishing for; the air is filled with snorts and ravenous noises. Even though they already have eaten more than their daily allotment, the animals fixate on wanting more, paying no mind to his pathetic appeal for attention.

Despite knowing their love of food, Tom's self-assurance is deeply affected by their lack of engagement with him, and his worrying over their feelings toward him worsens. He knows he must do something to rectify the situation and is willing to take drastic measures to return to their good side.

Nothing else matters but their acknowledgment and acceptance of his apology.

Tom makes another trip to the feed barrel, scoops up a small portion of food, and runs to the gate. He drops a few crumbles as he fumbles for the latch. Impatient that it's taking too much time to get inside the pen, he hops over the fence, and his boots make a loud *thud* as they hit the ground on the other side.

The pigs' gaze stays locked on the coffee can, and alas, Tom is still ignored.

He scans the pen, thinking their lack of care means they've decided in unison to snub him. Acting fast, he crawls on his hands and knees to join the rutting sows. Wedging his body into the cloister of animals, Tom becomes one with the herd.

Swiftly settling into a spot, he empties the contents of the can onto the dirt floor in front of him and, forcibly shoving the tip of his nose into the dirt, begins digging for each morsel. One by one, his tongue reluctantly licks the individual pieces from the ground, creating a muddy mixture of kernels in his mouth.

His cheeks hit their capacity, and he pauses to scan the others. Forcing his jaw to chew the combination of earth and the grit of the stiff pellets causes his teeth to ache.

Thrown off by the texture and sensation, he fights the urge to spit out the horrid concoction. As he chokes down the last bite, he gives a toothy grin, and his peeled-back lips showcase the dirt packed tightly between his teeth. Then, wanting the others' approval, he lets out a dry snort to communicate.

A single pig pushing against his body turns to look at him, nudges his rib cage, and snorts back. The small gesture is enough to give Tom the sense of community he's yearning for, and his growing smile reflects his replenishing confidence. As he watches the pig's head turning back to the ground to snuffle for food, a rush of warmth enters his racing heart.

Unable to contain his overwhelming love, he leans over to kiss its full belly, but just as his lips touch the sow's skin, he is stopped by a loud screech. The abrupt interruption causes a shattering sensation to ring through his ears, and every inch of his body freezes.

The barn's air is briefly filled with stagnant silence until heavy footsteps stomping against the concrete break the tranquility. Tom's heart races, and even though he wishes to clutch his chest to mute the bass-like thuds, he fears that if it is a violent intruder, any small motion may draw unwanted attention and put his life at risk.

Knowing he is not ready to die, he keeps his body stiff as a board, with his lips firmly pressed against the animal.

Unable to see what's going on from the angle of his compromised position, he fixates on the startling sounds. Their nondescript nature fuels his imagination, and he wonders if the apparitions of his grandparents have come back to reign terror over his simple life.

To calm himself, he glances up at the only thing that gives him stability—the pigs. Their noses continue rutting through the dirt. Not one appears to have an ounce of concern as they communicate with soft oinks.

Their nonchalant attitudes fill Tom with a sense of relief. As he reassures himself that his anxiety is fueling his fear, he takes a deep, calming breath and, with its exhalation, hears one last heavy footstep, then silence. Everything seems to return to normal.

Tom lifts his lips from the pig's skin, and as his facial muscles relax in preparation to laugh off the situation, something beats him to the punch.

It's the boisterous laughter of a man. Each deep cackle rings between the walls. "Isn't that just the weirdest sight you'll ever lay eyes on?" he says.

After chalking everything up to a misconception, Tom is thrown off by the voice, and the man's presence causes him to embark on a roller coaster of emotion.

The voice's deep, dominant tone makes Tom experience something he has never felt before: humiliation. Trying to escape the unpleasant feeling, he glances down at his palms. Of course, he doesn't understand how the situation could come across as wrong, but still, he is filled with an odd sense of shame.

The heavy footsteps begin again, but louder, as the man makes his way to the fence. Tom fights through his wave of confusion enough to recognize the short, stout man dressed in an off-white suit. It's the mayor.

As irritation stirs inside Tom, his fingers coil, gripping the dirt, and he forces a friendly smile onto his face. "I wasn't expecting to see you here.

So what's the occasion?" he asks. "You already congratulated me on my win, didn't you?"

The mayor smugly smirks and kicks the loose grain out of his path as he moves closer to the pen. The sound of the pellets sliding across the floor grabs the pigs' attention, and their ears perk up at the thought of receiving an additional snack.

Upon reaching the fence, the mayor slowly places his hands on the top railing and leans over it to look down at Tom. "Well, it's a little funny how I ended up here, but I sure am glad I did. I took a little tour around town to do my political duties like I usually do, and I saw your place and thought, you know what? That's where the winner of our pig jamboree lives. Then, as I drove by in my brand spanking new Cadillac, I noticed your barn door was left open. So, being the nice guy I am, I thought I should check on things and drove on in here as a courtesy. Never in my wildest dreams did I think I would encounter something as weird as this. I must say that this scene I just walked in on is nothing short of appalling," he says.

Tom doesn't like the idea of someone demeaning him and hides his growing rage by biting the insides of his cheeks. Knowing that the barn door isn't visible from the road, he senses the mayor is hiding something from him, and he plants his hands against the dirt to push himself onto his knees. "Oh, and why is that?" he asks.

The mayor lifts a single eyebrow. "We don't take fornication with animals lightly in this town," he says. "You know, from the moment I saw you in the back of that convertible, I knew you were odd."

Before he can continue, Tom bursts into maniacal laughter, and the lack of oxygen makes his face turn red as he tries to speak. "Really? I would have thought differently," he says.

Thinking he is being challenged, the mayor straightens his posture. "You questioning my judgment?" he asks.

The stern tone of the man's voice doesn't sit well with Tom. He slowly wipes his hands clean against his pants, and as his once-jovial expression fades, his temperament abruptly shifts to match the intruders.

Standing up, he notices a dried burgundy stain on the concrete near the mayor's boot. "All I'm saying is, you shouldn't be trespassing on another man's property. That's all," he says.

Every word sounds like a personal attack against the mayor's significance, and he is not used to his authority being challenged, so he is quick to react. His chest puffs out like a rooster, ready to fight. "Son, I advise you to know your place and watch your words. Remember that I run this town, and I can do as I please," he says.

Wanting to drive his point home, he walks toward the fence's gate to intimidate Tom. As he sets his hand on the latch, he spots Olive's hair in the crowded pen of pigs. "You know what? I'll make a deal with you. We can make a trade: the future of your reputation for that pig."

The idea of someone else touching his true love causes Tom's vision to blacken. Trying not to succumb to rage, he combats the surge of emotion by clenching his fists. "I told you once: I don't take kindly to trespassing. Don't make me tell you twice," he says.

Even though the mayor's strategy of intimidation is not working, he finds Tom's reaction comical, and with every word, he fights back a grin. Then, to push Tom's buttons further, the mayor fumbles to unchain the gate. "Well... maybe if you weren't patronizing with your pigs like some inbreed, you would have heard my car pulling in," he says.

One by one, Tom curls his fingers tighter into his palms, and his short nails cut his skin. "I never heard a car," he says.

Every clink of the metal chain clacking against the gate stings his ears. Tom's jaw clenches, and he grits his teeth. "Stop! Now!"

Thinking his discomfort is funny, the mayor smiles as he slowly finishes unlatching the entryway. Then, adding to the drama, he lifts his leg almost to his waist to exaggerate his intent to step inside the pen and, enjoying his moment of power, holds his foot in the air to antagonize Tom further.

Tom tightly coils his fists in a desperate attempt to ease his irritation. "I didn't hear Cadillac tires coming down the driveway," he says.

He is stuck on the idea, and the phrase echoes again and again in his mind. The thought of not hearing something that would be so blatantly obvious makes his eye twitch.

He can't help beating himself up over the blunder and is sure that he is the sole reason his precious pig's safety is at risk. "Stupid. You are stupid, just like everyone said you were," he says to himself repeatedly, his words persisting like the ticks of a time bomb preparing to detonate.

The spiraling behavior brings excitement to the mayor, and, like a lion's thrill when nipping at the heels of an antelope, he finds the same elation in pushing Tom to the edge of sanity.

He slows his boot's pace toward the dirt floor to prolong the torture.

One by one, the pigs feed off the noise of Tom's repetitive words, and, fueling the brewing chaos, they join in with high-pitched squeals. The room's energy intensifies as the commotion escalates, and together, its mash of sounds mimics a possessed choir amid an exorcism.

Tom borders on losing control as the noise compounds his negative feelings. Making one last attempt to derail the escalation, he squeezes his eyelids shut to stop the madness. "I said I didn't hear a car," he says louder.

His guttural tone brings on a bout of nausea that sweeps up his stomach and travels into his throat, charring the lining of his esophagus. The addition of the pigs' screams makes his head pulsate.

As much as he tries to focus, he cannot think, nor can he access his gut instinct to guide him on what to do next. Overwhelmed, he shouts at the top of his lungs. "There was no sound of wheels! I heard no wheels. Why are you lying to me?"

The aggressiveness behind his speech causes the mayor to become skittish, and, not sure he should proceed closer, he pauses, his foot hovering an inch away from the dirt as he glances in Tom's direction. The timbre of Tom's voice sounds foreign to him. After briefly processing the unsettling tone, he realizes he has never heard such a noise leave a grown man's mouth before.

The mayor's strained expression makes it hard to hide his internalized concern over what could surface next, and he knows that he must break the room's tension by forcing himself to appear more friendly. "Woah, there. Now, let's get a hold of ourselves. I told you all this could be cleared up with a simple trade, so I don't think it's necessary to act up over nothing," he says.

Tom is already too far gone to listen to this sad attempt at bargaining. As his swirling brain makes him motion-sick, he fights his urge to throw up by closing his eyelids. Left in darkness, his mind focuses on the horrendous pain of acid reflux as he rocks back and forth.

He shakes his head. "My pigs never made me feel this way. They are the only ones that truly care about me. Why did I listen to that woman? I shouldn't have left the barn."

Never having dealt with a situation where he's had to talk down someone emotionally unstable, the mayor's first instinct is to refrain from making sudden movements.

Sweat drenches his shirt as he closely watches Tom for trigger points. Feeling a knot slowly forming in his intestines, his foot instinctually begins to retract toward the concrete slab.

A tremor runs down Tom's arm and causes his fingers to twitch. It's like he's in another world.

The mayor panics. He has never witnessed cold-blooded rage like this in someone's eyes previously, and, frozen in terror, he fears he has provoked a response beyond his worst nightmares.

Paranoid that Tom has caught on to his snail-like escape, he covers his actions up with a nervous laugh. "You know what, Tom? I have an idea. Why don't we call this one big misunderstanding? Huh? I think that will make everyone feel better. Yep, this is all just one big misunderstanding," he says.

Tom's lack of responsiveness causes his speech to quicken and his tone to shift an octave higher. "If it makes you feel better, you are not crazy. The last thing I think you are is crazy." Letting out another laugh, he pretends to be making a joke with Tom rather than against him. "You know you sure are smart and have the hearing of a hawk. You were right about something: there weren't any tires. I had one of my pals from the jamboree drop me a bit down the road from your driveway so I could surprise you. So, you are not crazy... not crazy at all. You were right. There were no wheels."

Tom tries to tune out the noise. He grits his teeth and tilts his head from side to side, stretching his neck.

The mayor takes his movement as a good sign, and, believing his lies are working, he restarts his slow escape, moving his foot closer to the pen's exit.

Then, with a nervous chuckle, he continues. "It's a little inside joke we do to all the jamboree newcomers. So, now that you've been initiated, I'll cut to the chase: Welcome to the pig-showing community, pal. Well, I guess that means my duty is done, so I better get a move on. My friend should be looping around any minute now to pick me up," he says.

Tom's mouth springs open as if to gasp for air, and after a few heavy breaths, his eyes lock on the panicked man. It is as if his glare pierces his skin and into his soul.

Tom's vision goes black, and everything about the man standing before him looks different upon regaining focus. None of the mayor's attributes are identifiable. He can only see a man with an uncanny resemblance to his grandfather.

Abruptly, the noise plaguing his ears falls silent, and his vision tunnels. No matter how hard he tries to focus, he can only make out his grandfather's presence.

More than ready to face the man who continues to haunt him, he speaks. "It's you," he says in an eerie deep tone. His breathing becomes heavier, taking on the sound of a rattling air conditioner.

Tom's sinister voice frightens the mayor.

His body begins to shake uncontrollably, his knees buckle, and his hands jolt to grab onto the gate's frame to brace himself. His heart pounds loudly in his chest, and his eyes dart to Tom, then to the barn's exit, then back to Tom. Every ounce of color drains from his face upon seeing the loathing emanating from Tom like a spotlight. "Come on, pal. You know who it is. Would you look at that? I must say, it's getting awful late, so I'm gonna get going before it gets dark out."

Tom's vacant, unblinking stare makes the mayor feel he cannot be trusted, and without wasting another moment, he shifts his body to prepare to run for it.

His cowardly behavior strikes a nerve in Tom, and he stomps his foot. Upon getting the mayor's attention, he takes a deep inhalation of dust kicked up from his action. "Stop!"

The crispness of his voice rallies the pigs, and their teeth clack together while nipping at the air. Their chattering incisors sound like tiny hands clapping with applause for Tom's authoritative actions.

Hating that Tom is now in control, the mayor can't stop his competitive edge from surfacing. Still frozen and facing the opposite direction, he attempts to regain his superiority.

He turns his back to hide his quivering lip while his trembling fingers grasp harder around the fence pole. Clearing his throat, he attempts to stabilize his stammer and, unable to do so, mumbles, "Mhmm."

Tom's senses heighten, and his eyes widen with excitement. It's over ninety degrees outside, and the barn's uninsulated tin makes the interior a good ten degrees hotter. The heat and dust are stifling and escalate the room's intensity.

At once, he homes in on the sounds of the pigs' beating hearts and takes a step forward with a sense of empowerment. As his boot touches the ground, he is flooded with anger. "Why are you trying to take my pigs from me? Huh, Earl?" he asks.

The mayor quickly recognizes the name and chalks up the confrontation to Tom dealing with deep-seated abandonment issues. Thinking all he needs is a little comforting, he turns around and tries a different approach to de-escalate the situation. "Woah, now, Tom. You know it's me, the mayor, standing in front of you. Being the bigger man, I confess that maybe my little prank was distasteful."

The mayor chuckles. "You gotta admit, your reaction is a bit ridiculous, but I am willing to forgive and forget. We all know that lonesomeness can cause all types of crazy behaviors. So let's shake on putting this whole misunderstanding behind us," he says, and then, forcing a grin, he extends his hand. "What do you say? Let's let bygones be bygones?"

Tom picks at his fingernails and mumbles as he looks toward the ground. "You're not going to take my pigs from me. Do you hear me?" he says, sounding a bit despondent.

The mayor senses a softening in the boy's demeanor, giving him the confidence to re-assert his dominance. "I already told you, boy, this was just one big misunderstanding—nothing to worry your head about. Anyway, my friend should be back any minute to get me. I better head out to meet him so he doesn't come looking for me," he says.

Something about his demeanor doesn't sit well with Tom. While he watches the mayor's lips move, he only hears words of supremacy and threats of abandonment. His jaw clenches as he fights his emotion. "You aren't leaving until you listen to me!" he says.

The pigs' squeals ramp up louder around him. Amid the chaos, the mayor is oblivious to Olive's proximity as she gently takes the corner of his pant leg in her mouth.

Tom's radical shift in tone dumbfounds the mayor, and while trying to assess the situation, he notices a strange characteristic in Tom's eyes. Their lifeless nature and the excessive white below the pupils emanate psychopathy. It was something he hadn't picked up on earlier, but now, it is so apparent that the stare creates an off-putting feeling that digs deep into the mayor's gut.

Trying not to radiate his suspicions, the mayor slowly shifts his weight from one foot to another as he pivots toward the door. "Easy there, now, Tom. I'm going to let you get to your supper. I'm sure this whole thing will all blow over after a meal and a good night's rest," he says.

The terror in the mayor's voice sparks a wave of adrenaline in Tom. His lips curl into an ominous smile as he savors the moment of pleasure. He gives a quick nod that, if one were not in tune with the escalating situation, like the mayor, one might take as a sign of friendly agreement.

The mayor senses he has mitigated the hostile situation through his smooth exchange of words, and he lets out a long sigh to seal the deal. "I knew we could work things—"

Before the mayor can finish his statement, Tom glances at the surrounding pigs, his eyes reigniting with a peculiar glimmer. His family rallying around him makes him feel unstoppable, like a king ruling over his domain. "You heard the man," he says.

The pigs' beady eyes stare up at him, and their squeals become louder. Tom bites his lip in anticipation, and the thrill of it makes him snicker. "It's supper time," he says.

On cue, the pigs fall silent, and Olive latches more intently to the mayor's pants. Her body remains so still that the mayor, consumed by the tense situation, is oblivious to her teeth's restraining grip.

The sudden silence leaves the mayor confused. Although the lack of distraction should be beneficial for processing his thoughts, his mind goes blank as he works to devise a plan of escape.

Left without a single new idea and with a mind of mush, he pulls from what he knows: televised game shows. The mayor has watched them consistently, at every meal, for years. Being a bachelor, he enjoys the company as he eats in front of the television, shouting his answers and commiserating with the host over ridiculous contestants.

He raises his voice to get everyone's attention, just like he has seen on TV, but his skill set as a host is lacking, and the words tumble from his mouth, just like many of the contestants he frequently berates. "Wait. Huh? Pigs? Silence?" he says.

Caught off-guard by the deadened stares, he glances at the exit on the other side of the barn. "Awe, hell." The length looks further than before, and, already short of breath, he mentally prepares to run.

Even though the mayor thinks his behavior is cunning, Tom is one step ahead. "I should have known you small-minded men are all the same. You never even gave me a chance when I finally decided to share my talent as a pig farmer. Instead, all you care about is tormenting people like me."

His demeanor tenses at the thought of everyone leaving the jamboree over false accusations of him cheating. "Selfish, selfish, selfish," he says.

Realizing that the situation has taken a turn for the worse, the mayor knows he must bolt toward the sliding barn door, but something pulling on his pant leg stops him dead in his tracks as he attempts his first step.

Thinking the material has caught on the fence, he worries that he will snag his favorite power suit. As he reluctantly looks down to ensure he's not damaging his ensemble, his gaze is met with something completely unexpected.

It's Olive. Her teeth are latched on to his polyester fabric for dear life.

The mayor feels trapped. His eyes widen with panic as he frantically kicks his leg to free himself, but his efforts are futile, making his blood run ice-cold through his veins.

With each kick, Olive's jaw locks tighter on the ivory material, and rather than giving up, her head jerks from left to right to make him submit. Then, with growing aggression, her thick belly lowers to the ground, and she rolls like an alligator trying to subdue its prey.

The mayor struggles to stand. His strategy flips from talking his way out of the situation to fleeing for his life. He knows he must keep himself upright if he wants a chance to escape.

Pools of sweat stain his underarms and drip from his forehead. He frantically grabs at the sides of the gate to stabilize himself, but with Olive's aggressive pulling, his hands are barely able to get even a partial grip.

He shouts for Tom's help, but his frantic state causes his words to translate into anger. "Don't just stand there, you idiot! Get your damn pig off me!" He shouts.

Tom pays no attention to the mayor's harsh tone; the sounds of the heightened pleas make his lips twitch with excitement. Feeling that the scene could use a few more elements, he shrieks a high-pitched yell, calling the remaining pigs to join in. "Woo, wee pigs! Suey!"

In response, the pigs squeal at the top of their lungs. Abiding by the command, they crowd to join Olive like a swarm of bees frantic to return to their hive.

They bask in the addictive aroma of the mayor's salty perspiration as they approach. Then, with loud, snarling grunts, they grab onto any bit of cloth or loose skin with their gnashing teeth, locking onto him like a frenzied school of piranhas.

In unison, they work to overpower him, dragging his body down to their level. As the mayor fights to combat the multi-directional pull, his throbbing limbs attempt to grasp the edges of the railing for dear life.

The hostility of the jerking movements on his lower body worsens, and in rebuttal, his grip tightens. The violent friction of his tender skin rubbing against the metal causes the flesh to peel from his soft palms.

He knows he can't hold on much longer as the pain overtakes him. He screams, and the horrifying sounds of desperation leaving his mouth match the tenacity of the squealing sows as they fight over his flesh. "Please, get them off me. I mean... you can't do this to me. I'm the mayor!"

His screams become more deafening. "Don't just stand there. Help me, you dumb shit!"

Tom chuckles and shakes his head as he watches the pigs give one last tug that rips the mayor from the fence. "You aren't the mayor, Earl," he says.

The mayor's breath is knocked out of his lungs as he hits the dirt floor. Enjoying the sight, Tom slowly approaches to get a better look at the specks of red collecting on Olive's long coat.

"You know, Earl, everyone wonders how my pig's fur got to be like it is," he says. Then, with a laugh, he continues. "Lucky for you, the cat's out of the bag. It's funny that you are the only living person, besides me, who knows my special recipe—the secret sauce. I'm sure you are thinking, why didn't I think of that? Too bad you didn't find out sooner. You could have tried it too, but with one foot in the grave, it's probably a little late for that Earl."

Each of the pigs' little snorts mimics his snickering. Tom lowers himself into a squat behind the feasting herd.

As he settles into a comfortable position, he notices the oddly untainted cowboy boots sticking out beneath the pink pigs' bellies and finds them calling his name. Tom glances down at the belt buckle between his hips and the cream-colored cowboy boots on the mayor's feet. "Hey, mayor, what's your shoe size?" he asks.

While gasping for breath, the mayor attempts to make one last plea for help, but his bloodcurdling cries are preempted by Olive's teeth ripping through his throat. The fresh wound severs his jugular, causing blood spurts to pulse into the air with every heartbeat.

Tom remains nonchalant as he sits down on the dirt and picks up where the conversation had left off with his new buddy. "Actually, no need to respond. I know you got a lot going on over there. This is an easy fix," he says.

He lifts his leg to compare the length of the boot's soles. "See, I can figure this one out on my own." With a glance, he can see that the two are roughly similar in size, and, briefly tapping them together sole to sole, he decides it is worth the effort to salvage them.

He softens his voice as he reaches to take them from the mayor's feet. "Don't worry now, mayor; I promise these will go to a great home." Then, swiftly, with two quick pulls, he plucks the boots from the dying man's feet and smiles.

Two outlier pigs, each a bit smaller than the rest, lift their snouts to smell the air, and their noses pick up an enticing stench. As they follow the aroma, they notice the man's bare, twitching toes, and their squeals ramp with hunger. They look at one another, then lunge toward the mayor's feet to fight for the newly uncovered delicacies.

A scuffle ensues, and Tom scoots backward to protect himself and the prized cowboy boots from the blood bath.

Smitten with his findings, he huddles near the water trough, ogling the leather's fine details. "Woo-wee, these sure are pretty," he says. Then, holding them in front of his face, he swivels the boots in a circular motion to admire them from each angle as he tunes out the chaos surrounding him. "Saved you just in the nick of time."

The sight of them makes it impossible for him to contain his excitement, and, allowing his impatience to win, he starts to take off his shoes to try the boots on. As one boot dangles halfway off his foot, he hears a vehicle in the distance, and his ears perk up to listen.

Even though it still sounds relatively far away, it is as loud as a monster truck, making it a bit more difficult to estimate its proximity. Irritated by the noise, Tom stops what he's doing. "Well, if that's not a perfect addition to the day's events," he says. The thought of an interruption stretches his patience thin and puts him in a bad mood. "Looks like your good ole' friends didn't forget about you, after all, mayor!"

Shouting across the pigsty, his face grows red. "Everyone just wants to rain on our parade today, don't they, Olive?" Tom momentarily sits in silence as he tries to pinpoint the location of the noise by focusing on the engine's rumble. As he listens, he gathers a rough estimate of how much time remains before the company arrives. He then frustratingly looks at the new boots and becomes annoyed that he has to postpone trying them on due to another unwelcome visitor.

The large truck slows to turn into his long driveway, and the sound of the sputtering engine grows louder. The noise makes Tom spring to his feet, realizing that he had seriously misjudged the timing of their arrival.

He grabs the new shoes by the leather loopholes and hops on one leg to finish wedging his heel back in his shoe. Then, not allowing himself even a moment to breathe, he sprints across the pen and jumps over the fence. The minute his boots touch the concrete, he runs to the wooden cabinet that holds the pigs' grooming tools, tosses his new prized possessions inside, and slams the cabinet door shut.

Tom knows from his prior mental timing of the pig's feasting habits that, depending on the body size, his group can devour anything in roughly ten minutes. As he tries not to get worked up over the rapid dissipation of time, he tells himself everything will be fine. With barely a second to spare, he glances back at the horde of feasting pigs to check their progress.

Only a tiny portion of the mayor's pelvis is left. They are almost finished, but it's a bloody mess. His struggle to fight back is evidenced by the red spatters covering the pigs' bodies. Although most of what's left of the mayor's body matter has pooled in a pile of sloshy goop, it still decorates a more significant section of the dirt floor than usual.

Tom paces, trying to find the silver lining. "Shit. Well, at least none of it got on the concrete," he says.

His eyes look to the sun, which he can see beginning to set through the partially open sliding barn door. Stopping to listen, he checks for the car's progress. The sound lets him know he only has moments left.

Knowing his ensuing choices will dictate his future, his eyes anxiously dart back to the door. "No going back now," he says.

Chapter Nine

PIGS LOVE TOMATOES

The pigs' hunger is slowing down. Their grinding mouths are losing steam after eating both later than usual and a heaping extra portion.

Tom shifts gears, and his eyes dart to the crimson splatters across the animals' bodies and ground. "Think, think, think," he says.

One of the pigs spots the sparkling water sloshing to the brim in the oblong water trough and slowly waddles toward it. Tom's mind sparks an idea.

He races to the water-filled container, beating the animal to the punch, and while remaining on the concrete, he firmly grabs hold of the trough's metal lip. His fingers tingle as a wave of strength accompanies his grip, and, sounding a grunt, he tips it over.

At first, the pig stops and appears disappointed, then oinks with glee as the water rushes between its feet. Hearing the commotion, the rest of the herd's attention turns to the tsunami of water gushing toward them.

Pulled from their thoughts of feasting, the sight reminds them of their dehydration from the barn's heat and their continuous gorging. They lick their lips and flock to stick their snouts in the muddy stream, and within mere seconds, the blood spattering their faces is replaced with darkened sludge.

Even though their pen is a decent size, the water touches every inch of it, flooding the space, and the pigs' stomping feet and rooting noses instantaneously turn it into a mud pit.

Olive is the last one to finish eating, and, hearing the ruckus, she pulls her snout away to survey the cause of the excitement. The scene of frolicking fills her with exhilaration, and she joins in, tromping in circles and creating a muddy spot. She lowers her body to the ground and rolls around on her back, wildly kicking her feet in the air.

As Tom regards the scene of the entire herd joining in on the rolling fun and getting covered in mud, he revels in his brilliance.

At the same time, the truck rolls into the barnyard, and for the most part, the engine falls silent. However, its poor tuning causes it to spit out a few sputters after the key is turned, reminding the occupants of the barn that the visitors have indeed arrived.

It causes Tom to snap back to the reality of the situation, and he is thrust into fight-or-flight mode, knowing that there are only seconds left before he will have to deal with the unwelcome guest.

His neck jars to scan the area where the mayor's body once lay. Only minor remnants of flesh, splintered bone fragments, and a bit of gut matter have been left behind.

The truck's heavy door slowly opens a short distance from the barn's entrance, and the hinges let out a creak.

In a swooping dance, Tom spins to the two pitchforks hanging from the wall and, grabbing one, sprints to the pen's open gate. Stepping inside, he latches the entrance behind him. It's ideally timed, coinciding with the loud *thud* of the truck's door shutting.

While several pigs play contentedly in the mud, one almost steps into the crime scene. Tom jumps into action, utilizing the backs of the rusted prongs to swat at the animals, shooing them away from the area. His shoulders shake off a jitter as he regains his composure. He rakes the site using the pointed ends, sifting through the soppy mess and shaking the prongs with every scoop, hoping to appear as if he is cleaning up feces. Drips of sweat fall from his hairline as he works while whistling the tune of Old McDonald.

The awaited footsteps land on the concrete inside the entrance, followed by stagnant silence.

Tom's perspiration worsens, causing drops of sweat to soak his clothes and drip from his forehead onto the toes of his boots. He tries to act normal, but his voice trembles as he hums the happy melody. Unable to control his nerves, he senses an oncoming tremor traveling from the base of his arms to his hands, and he tightens his grip around the work tool to prevent its arrival.

The footsteps pick up their movement across the concrete floor, but the pattern is confusing. It is uneven, giving the impression that whomever the individual is, they have a stagger to their steps.

Tom continues to pretend to work and refrains from looking up to satisfy his curiosity.

A loud crash sounds; someone has collided with the tin feed can, and inside the tin barn, every little bang and rattle turns into an obnoxious echo as the lid spins to settle flat against the hard ground.

The pigs rolling and cooling their bodies in the wet dirt respond to the noise with high-pitched squeals.

Tom flinches and instinctively glances up. Recognizing his unintentional movement a little too late, he defensively forces a smile onto his face to greet the intruder. "Can I help you?" he asks.

A man lies sprawled across the ground, dressed in a dirty, mint-green work shirt, grass-smudged jeans, and tan-colored work boots. The can's lid rests beside him on the cold concrete floor.

The man's position makes it impossible for Tom to identify him, and, not receiving an immediate response, he is forced to wait, staring at the light brown hair on the back of the man's head.

Roughly five minutes pass of the guy lying in the same position. The pigs lose interest due to their short attention spans and go back to playing in the mud. Tom refrains from blinking while closely monitoring the man's limbs for any sign of life, and the lapse of time causes his eyes to dry.

He becomes annoyed and impatient over the uneasiness brought on by the stranger's presence. Wanting him to leave, he tries to speed things up by loudly clearing his throat to provoke movement, but after he finishes, he is met with silence and morbidly wonders if the man is dead. After waiting another moment to be proven wrong, he witnesses no sudden change, and the body's stiffness relieves him.

Not having to deal with another intruder that day is preferable, and, believing he does not have to worry about the man rising and walking around the barn, Tom allows himself to succumb to his tiredness. He leans the pitchfork against the fence, but as he stretches his arms above his head, he hears a thunderous snore exit the man's throat.

The stranger begins hacking to catch his breath. Caught by surprise, everything regarding the turn of events triggers a bout of anger in Tom. "Of course, nothing can be simple," he says.

For a moment, he goes along with his pessimistic thoughts but swiftly stops himself before he is overtaken by negativity. He clenches his back molars together to mitigate any oncoming outbursts and fights not to roll his eyes.

Rerouting his patience, he inhales a deep breath, reminding himself that he has yet to learn the man's intentions. Then, slowly, he forces himself to repeat his greeting. "Can I help you?"

The sound of Tom's irritated yell helps kickstart the stranger's reorientation process, and as he starts to regain consciousness, his eyes flutter open to see who's speaking. Seeing no one standing directly in front of him, his head lifts from the floor, and he peers around to examine his surroundings.

At first glance, he concludes that he's in a barn, and, feeling he has checked one item off his list of questions, his confusion shifts to his body's odd positioning. He can't help wondering how he ended up on the floor. His arms flail by his sides until finally settling in a position to help him sit up.

"Mmmm, hmm... yeah," he says. Nothing makes sense, and his words jumble together. His palms flatten against the ground to better stabilize him, and he reaches for the open grain bin beside him to use as a crutch to help himself stand.

Tom's pupils move back and forth as he watches the stranger's weight sway the giant grain-filled metal trashcan from side to side. Trying to hold his patience together, he winces each time it is on the verge of tipping.

"I said, can I help you?'" he asks again.

The man realizes the voice is coming from behind him, and, in anticipation of turning around, he extends his hand to point at Tom upon completing his pivot. "You that guy with the long-haired pig?" he asks as his disoriented body swivels.

Tom glances at Olive, covered in mud, and waits for a sign from her about how to respond before returning his gaze to meet the stranger's eyes. "Depends on who's asking," he says.

With a few staggering steps, the man stumbles forward, trips over the grain bin lid, and, pretending to act as if nothing happened, uses the fence railing in front of Tom to catch his fall.

He slowly straightens his posture, looking down at Tom. He enjoys that the concrete slab adds a few inches to his height; it makes him feel superior. "Well, I should be asking you the same question," he says.

Tom smirks at the stranger's slurred sarcasm upon realizing, after catching a whiff of moonshine, that his issues are not because of his fall but rather the cause of his fall. He is entertained by the idea of an intoxicated man trying to outwit him at his own game and decides to inquire further. "Is that so?" he asks.

Immediately, the man nods, and the dramatic nature of the movement causes him to lose his balance. He leans over the fence, and his eyes scan the pen. "Say, you happen to see the mayor wandering around in here?" he asks.

With a shrug, Tom follows his gaze to the muddy area. "Looks like there are only pigs in here to me. So, guess you have your answer," he says.

Pausing for a moment, the man scans the pen again. "Huh, well, maybe you're right," he says. Tom fights back a chuckle. Perplexed, the stranger backs off from the railing to teeter on his own.

The encounter appears too easy, but Tom takes it as a stroke of good luck. "Nice of you to stop by," he says.

With a half-nod, the man turns to leave, then stops as he catches a clear view of the pitchfork Tom had been using to clean the pen. His hand gestures to the red residue coating the bottom part of the handle and the tines. "Say, you hurt yourself on that or something?" he asks.

Thrown off by the question, Tom responds without thinking. "Nope, not sure why you would think that," he says. As he finishes his answer, he observes the man's eyes squinting to get a better view of the ground by his feet.

The stranger moves back to the fence to take a closer look. "That sure looks like blood to me," he says. He surveys the surrounding ground with a skeptical expression and gives Tom another scan. "You sure the mayor didn't stop by?" he asks.

Tom glances at the pitchfork and spots what the man is referencing—a thick red chunky substance coating the forks. Trying not to seem suspicious, he finds himself fumbling for words to redirect the conversation. "Oh, that mess. I can see how you may think it's from an injury, but it's remnants of tomatoes," he says as he shifts the position of the tool to a closer angle.

The man's pupils dart to the sharpened ends as Tom flips the pitchfork over, leaving the prongs pointing up. "Tomato?" he asks with doubt.

"Yep, that's the secret to growing hair on a pig: tomatoes," Tom says as he uses the tip of his finger to swipe a scoop of slurry off one of the tines. He holds his breath and, fighting back the urge to vomit, licks it from his finger with a smile. "See?" he says.

His rapid speech makes the man slightly suspicious. He intently watches Tom's every move, but his pleasant expression shakes his worry. "Tomatoes sure are good this time of year," he says.

Then, being a nosy man, he scans Tom's appearance, and his eyes widen when he catches sight of his belt buckle. "Say, where did you get that mighty fine pig buckle?"

Tom's skin becomes clammy. "I won it," he says, "at the pig jamboree."

His response makes the man's eyebrows lift. "I thought they stopped that tradition some years back?" he asks.

Tom is quick to poke a hole in his story. "Did you compete this year?" he asks. The stranger shakes his head. "Then how would you know?"

The question strikes a nerve, and the man's jaw muscles pulsate as he clenches his teeth. "My brother was the last to win one," he says.

Connecting the dots, Tom strokes his chin as if pondering a distant memory. "You know, now that you mention it, the mayor told me earlier at the pig jamboree that my buckle looked similar to one owned by some guy in town who went missing. Go figure—wouldn't that be a strange coincidence if he was referring to your brother? Such a small world it is," he says.

Knowing he should come off as sorrowful, Tom pauses, drops his shoulders, and shifts his expression to one of condolence. By giving the man the best look of sympathy he can muster, he hopes the emotional display will ease any doubts and get him to leave. "For what it's worth, I'm sorry for your loss."

The man couldn't care less about what Tom was saying. Continuing to fixate on the buckle, he spots some odd scratch marks, and his suspicions solidify.

He has made up his mind about Tom. As a stubborn-minded man, he trudges forward, ready with his accusations. "The mayor was right. You did something to him, didn't you?" he says. With no intention of hearing Tom's answer, his hands wrap around the fence posts to simulate wringing his neck.

Tom slowly lifts a hand to calm him. "As I said, I don't know your brother. I never met the man, and I will answer your other question once more to save you from wasting your time. I haven't seen the mayor since the fairgrounds, so there is no reason for you to be here looking for him. So that's that," he says while straightening his posture.

"Now that you have all your answers, I'd say it's getting late. You have overstayed your welcome." As he finishes speaking, his grip tightens around the pitchfork's handle.

Still fixated on the possibility of revenge, the man refuses to budge.

Chuckling, he stares into the distance, thinking of how the day unfolded. "There I was, minding my own business, having my usual drink at the local haunt, and the mayor came in all wild-eyed, looking like he just saw a ghost," he says.

As he takes a moment to reminisce further, his hands become animated, adding a dramatic effect to the second half of his story. "You know, he told me that he thought you knew what may have happened to my brother, but I didn't believe the guy at first."

He glances back at Tom to read his expression. "I mean, who would? The man told this outlandish tale about a pig with hair, which we all know is bizarre enough on its own to tank the entire claim of knowing where my brother is."

The mention of Olive causes Tom's forehead to perspire, and he immediately worries that the stranger could be making up the whole story of being the dead buffoon's brother. There is only one thought plaguing his mind: *What if it's only a ploy to steal my pig, just like the mayor?*

As the idea digs in deeper, it makes him nervous, and he sneaks a peak at Olive to ensure she is safe. The sight of her matted mud-soaked hair gives him a sense of relief. Even though she is still beautiful to him, her coat's luster is masked, and he knows that her concealed identity will protect her from becoming a target. Feeling confident in her safety, he looks at the stranger and laughs, "That sounds ridiculous. There is no such thing as a pig with hair."

The laughter provokes a wave of anger in the stranger. He can sense that Tom is hiding something and wants to get to the bottom of it. His eyes immediately dart to the pen and scan each of the pigs. "I already said that everyone knows that. The only thing that had my attention was the mention of my brother's whereabouts. So, I took the mayor's offer of a few drinks for a ride out here. I thought there was nothing to lose," he says.

Taking a moment to sniffle, he sucks a single tear back inside his ducts, and his face turns red. "I don't care about no pig. All I care about is getting justice for good ole Danny Boy."

As if praying, Tom lifts his hand to gesture his commiseration. "Don't we all?" he says.

With a clenched fist, the man hits the fence railing and points at Tom. "Shut your trap! I'm not
finished," he says.

The noise of ringing metal upsets the pigs, and
they loudly squeal. Tom cringes. Nothing irks him
more than hearing the poor animals upset. "Lower
your tone," he says.

Danny Boy's brother doesn't heed the command,
and his fists clench so tightly that his knuckles
turn a shade of white. He can no longer control
his anger, and as it boils to the surface, he loses
all control. "I ought to just come in there right
now and wring your skinny neck," he says. His
rage continues to escalate, and he charges down
the fence.

"Mayor or not, I'm going to finish what he was
supposed to." He confirms his intentions, aggressively stepping toward the gate. "You are a dead
man, Tom! You hear me? Dead!"

Still wobbly from the alcohol, he stumbles. His
palms grasp the fence to catch his fall, and pausing
for a moment; he glances up to the ceiling. "This
one's for you, Danny Boy."

Tom is confused and looks up to see whom he
is talking to. But, not seeing anyone, he remains
solid in his stance, paying close attention to how
the situation unfolds.

Although the man spews fighting words, his
movements are executed with a lagging nature
and don't align with his threats. Tom can tell the

grown man is not mentally astute, and he stays one step ahead by taking advantage of it.

Noticing the man's knees holding a slight bend as if ready to leap, Tom lunges forward with his pitchfork in hand and, keeping a tight grip on the handle, wedges it into the mud, leaving the prongs pointing upward.

As the stranger gains adrenaline, he straightens his knees and shouts a warriorlike yell while springing over the fence.

Tom braces himself as the man's flying body perfectly impales itself on the jagged metal prongs, and the sound of it spearing through the man's soft skin and the cartilage of his torso feeds his power. Then, fighting to keep the man's flailing body from knocking him over, he tightens his grip and widens his stance.

As each sharp prong slowly slices through the man's gut and travels toward his spine, his body goes limp. The rusted object digs deeper in the direction of the bone, and the pointed ends stretch the skin on his back thin as if wanting to break through.

To Tom's ears, the gruesome orchestration of crackling noises from the impact mimics wrapping paper peeling off a gift on Christmas Day, and he relishes it in a deep state of euphoria. Basking in the sensation, he closes his eyes as his nostrils widen to smell the fresh stench of iron.

Tom revels in the sounds from the heckling pigs and grins.

The heaviness of the man's limp body continues to push the jagged, dagger-like ends through his flesh, and the residual noise of each cracking rib and vertebra echoes between the walls of the tin barn.

As Tom reopens his eyes, he meets face-to-face with the man's glare. Enjoying the view, he stares deep into his pupils during the last moments of his life, fixating on the glint leaving his eyes.

Blood trickling from his lip onto his chin causes Tom's muscles to tense with a vengeance, and his grip releases from the pitchfork, letting the man's body fall to the mud.

The sloshing thud catches the pig's attention, and they ogle his twitching fingers.

Tom leans forward and grabs the pitchfork with a chuckle. "I hope everyone saved room for dessert," he says.

His hands slowly tighten around the wooden handle, and, preparing to pull, he notices that the body's catawampus positioning has rattled something out from beneath the man's shirt. As he gives a hefty yank, he tries to get a closer look at the shiny object hanging around his neck. "Huh, how did I miss that?" he says.

As he frees the blades from the man's torso, the small intestine follows. While still fixating on the object's shine, Tom complacently cleans the guts off the spear's edges in the mud, then leans the tool against the fence.

As he moves back toward the body, a pig on the outskirts of the feasting earlier seizes its moment to be the first in line and lunges at the corpse with a loud snort.

Tom panics. Not having had a chance to decide whether he wants the enticing object from the man's body, his instincts kick in, and he angrily snorts to show dominance. Rushing at the small sow, he flails his arms to scare it off. "Get out of here! Get! Get! Now get!" he says.

The boisterous act creates no effect, and ignoring him, the pig carries on with its feast. Grabbing the first thing in sight, it aggressively attacks the stray intestine next to the body. Even though Tom is relieved by her choice, but still worries that the object dangling from the stranger's neck may be next. Rather than making another attempt to scare her off, he goes into salvage mode and jumps forward, his limbs extended straight out in front of him, sliding belly-first through the mud to beat the others to the man's head. Without bothering to assess it first, he quickly removes the object and clutches it in his fist.

As the pig finishes slurping down the intestine, Tom's closeness to the meat causes it to squeal at the top of its lungs. Possessive over its meal, the animal lays claim to the feast, and, challenging him, it takes a snarling step forward.

Unbothered by the threat, Tom, drenched from head to toe in mud, ignores the danger and attempts to shoo the pig away. "Yeah, yeah, stop your complaining. I'm not bothering anything," he says as he walks toward the gate.

Looping the piece of gold jewelry around his fingers, he holds it up to the lighting and immediately takes a liking to the circular pendant, which has the imprint of a tiny pig footprint stamped in the middle. He smiles from ear to ear. "You did good, Tom. Real good," he says.

Feeling something pinch his calf, he spins around to see what's going on and is met with the angry stare of the same animal that he'd just watched suck down the intestine. It appears crazed as it stands behind him. Blood stains the pig's lower jaw, and, continuing to snarl, it charges again toward him, but this time when it bites, its teeth sink into his skin.

The thrill of tasting something living makes it ravenous as it licks its lips, thinking of its next taste.

Tom's reflexes take over, and he kicks at the voracious creature. "I said get!" he says.

The pig considers his action a part of the hunting game, and it lunges at his legs to bite them. Flustered by the odd behavior, Tom snaps and angrily kicks at it with all his might. A single heavy blow hits the animal's ribs, and the momentum causes its body to roll through the mud.

Without remorse, Tom sternly points to the rest of the pigs, who are still devouring the corpse. "That's the food, you stupid pig, not me," he says.

Picking itself up from the ground, the animal has vengeance in its beady eyes and glares at him with hatred. As it takes a breath, the pain Tom inflicted causes it to squeal, slowly returning to the feeding frenzy.

Tom calmly secures his new piece of jewelry around his neck as he walks toward the gate. After proudly stepping onto the concrete slab, he turns and fastens the chain behind him.

"You pull some shit like that again, and you'll be next," he says. He laughs while his eyes continue to glare in the biting pig's direction. "You aren't the important one. Olive is. *You* are disposable."

Tom shakes his head and walks to the grooming cabinet to grab his new boots. Holding them in his hand, he stares at the overturned trough and snickers. "Since it seems like some of us have forgotten our place, we will use this as a lesson so that it never happens again."

He swings the boots to motion for the pigs to pay attention, then raises his voice to make an announcement. "Thanks to your little friend, no one gets water until morning."

The pigs squeal with anguish.

Tom cynically glares back at the devilish pig that bit him and motions his head for the others to look. "Yup, do what you want with him," he says.

As he walks to the barn's exit, he smirks at the sounds of the animal's pleas. "Now, because I need to get used to married life, I'm retiring to the house for the night. That means no more of our little slumber parties. No ifs, and, or buts—that's where I'll be from now on. I expect everyone to be on their best behavior for the remainder of the night and for that man's mess to be gone by morning."

The pigs squeal for his attention.

Ignoring their cries, Tom is enthralled by the sensation of control. As he whistles the happy tune of Old McDonald, he makes his exit, cowboy boots in hand, and slides the door shut behind him.

Chapter Ten

SUFFOCATED

Outside, the crickets chirp as the stars twinkle through the darkness that has overtaken the sky. The serenity of the night makes everything seem peaceful.

Or at least, that's what Tom wants to believe.

But the noises of the chirping insects repeatedly remind him of his pig's crying squeals, and his swirling thoughts continually contradict the night's calming ambiance.

As the memory of the pigs' facial expressions replays in his mind, he can't shake the vivid details of their heated exchange, which worsens his anxiety. Standing in the darkness, the nagging chirping of the crickets magnifies his guilt by reminding him that the pigs have been left alone in the lightless barn.

The evening's atmosphere grows louder around him. Tom swings his arms wildly in every direction to make it stop, and, tired of feeling shame, he employs his pride to redirect his thoughts. "They have to learn. It's called tough love. If they don't have consequences, they will never listen," he says as he takes a few more steps.

Realizing he has already passed the edge of the barn, he spots where the stranger had sneakily parked his gray truck around the corner to hide it from view. The last thing he wants to do is deal with any more chaos, and he rolls his eyes.

Wanting to be done for the night, he continues to walk toward the farmstead. As he tries to ignore the truck's presence, he feels someone watching him, and he shivers. Consumed by paranoia, he continues to walk, staring straight ahead, until something stops him dead in his tracks—a pulsating light emanating through the front window from the kitchen.

Initially, he chalks the odd visual display up to his exhaustion, but as he rubs his eyes, every room in the home's light fixtures joins in the surge. As each of the pulsing illuminations becomes more robust, the first floor's large picture window frames the flashing outline of a woman's silhouette. The backlighting shows her frame floating in the direction of the kitchen, and every movement she makes draws attention to her nightgown flowing fluidly behind her.

Although her whimsical nature entices Tom, he is weary after his previous experience within the walls of the farmstead. He wants to verify whether Claudia has decided to surprise him or his grandmother has returned, so he squints to assess the details of the female presence.

Feeding off his curiosity, the figure travels to the middle of the window frame, pauses, and turns to face him. It tilts its head to match his look of confusion while making a single pass with its hand in a sweeping gesture. The fluidity of the motion causes goosebumps to travel down Tom's arm, and something about the presence immediately doesn't sit well with him. As his hair stands to a prickle, he feels his anxiety flush his skin. "It's only an illusion. That's all it is. It's your house. Remember, they have no power over you," he says.

After taking a deep breath, he resumes his approach but seeing the figure remain resolute in its position and confident it is not Claudia, his nerves get the best of him.

With an abrupt turn, he changes his trajectory, moving in the direction of the truck. "You know what? I bet they will be gone by the time you return, and that's that."

The light breeze carries the sounds of the pigs rummaging in their pen. Tom's stress builds from his guilt triggered by the noise, and he picks up his pace.

As he gets closer to the vehicle, his eyes narrow to see through the darkness. The area where the truck is parked is surrounded by trees, making it darker than the rest of the barnyard. He extends his arms to feel for the driver's-side door. "It'll be best if I get this done tonight," he says nervously. "Should have done it during daylight. That's what I get for procrastinating."

Regardless of how much he tries to convince himself he's making the right choice, he still feels slightly unsure of his decision, and as he fumbles in his pitch-black surroundings, he tries to think of something positive. "I have to get rid of this thing sooner or later. Got to hide it before Claudia returns. There's no way around it."

Abruptly, the wind ceases, and the pigs go silent in the barn.

The drastic fluctuation in noise fuels Tom's unrest. As his mind tries to create sounds to fill the dead-quiet atmosphere, he becomes certain he hears something fiddling with the barn's sliding door as if trying to open it. Allowing himself to spiral with the wild idea, his breathing becomes heavy, and he jerks his head around to look. His eyes dart over the exterior of the dark tin structure.

Nothing is there, and the door remains closed.

To minimize his nerves, Tom attempts to make light of the situation, and as he chuckles at his skittishness, his free hand touches the truck's handle. When he pulls it open, the car's interior sounds a rhythmic beeping, bringing him a sense of relief. "Well, at least his drunken lack of common sense made him forget to take the damn keys out of the ignition," he says.

Still feeling like something is watching him, he wastes no time hopping inside. As he closes the door, he takes a deep breath, swiftly hits the locks, and chucks his new cowboy boots onto the passenger's side seat. Tom turns the key to start the engine and settles in as he listens to the soothing rumble purr in his ears. Calmed by the white noise, he feels safer and cranks up the heat to rid his arms of goosebumps.

As the warm air circulates through the cab, the radio suddenly starts blaring the last station it was left on. A heavy bass beat shakes the seats, followed by screaming metal vocals.

The words describe revenge.

While trying to orient himself to the unfamiliar vehicle, Tom is forced to listen to the first verse. The song's essence, paired with the aggressive pounding, triggers him, jolting him to the edge of stability.

Unable to take another moment, he dives across the seat and flips off the sound. Then, returning to the driver's side, he straightens his posture and checks his appearance in the rearview mirror.

He tries to use his familiarity to recenter his thoughts, but something is awry. His skin looks far older than his age. It's like his grandfather is staring back at him. Unable to look away, his hands grasp the steering wheel for support.

He can't move and is paralyzed by his anxiety.

Cutting through the eerie silence, a jolt of static comes over the radio, and the song resumes where it had left off. Tom feels the air blowing on his knuckles turn ice-cold, and his grip tightens around the steering wheel.

Tom fights the urge to look down, hoping that normalcy will return if he fixates on his eyes in the mirror while ignoring everything else. As he maintains a stagnant expression, he tries to reassure himself that everything is ok.

"You are nothing like him. Do you hear me? Nothing," he says.

The music's bass gradually turns up and plays louder, jingling the truck's metal frame. Tom's heart's pounding rhythm matches the song's beat, and the increased pressure in his chest cavity causes him to worry that the organ may explode if it persists.

His eyes flutter as he fills with panic. Slowly, it becomes harder for him to focus on his pupils in the mirror, and as he breaks his gaze, he watches in horror as the tip of his nose lengthens. Using every bit of surrounding skin, it expands into a cylindrical shape on his face, stretching several inches, painfully pulling the flesh of his cheeks and chin taut as it takes the form of a snout. Two small divots appear on its facing and then painfully burst open, forming nostrils. Unable to smell or breathe, he feels like he is suffocating through the transformation.

Running out of free skin to take, little by little, the whites of his irises are pulled in with the snout, leaving only the blackness of two beady pupils. He can no longer see his lips, and, desperately wanting to hear himself speak, he tries to pry open the skin where his mouth should be.

While his throat attempts to release a muffled, raspy croak, Tom uses his dull fingernails to slice his skin under his new snout to provide the semblance of a mouth, and, with the new opening, he inhales a gasping breath.

As he looks with panic into his rearview mirror, something slaps the glass of the passenger side window. It almost sounds like the whack of a giant's palm. In a chain reaction, Tom trembles uncontrollably, and even though he would rather not, he turns his head to look.

Nothing is there but the pitch-black abyss.

Tom worries that if he continues to stare, he may see something alarming, and, avoiding his terror-filled imagination, he turns back to check his reflection in the rearview mirror. Everything appears normal, but after the earlier ordeal, he is not entirely convinced by his reflection; he wants to double-check its accuracy.

As his hand adjusts the mirror to get a better look at the lower half of his face, he catches a glimpse of something moving in the truck's bed, and, not wanting to see what it is, he over-adjusts the rearview mirror toward the ceiling. Horrific moans stem from behind the cab, and the stress-provoking noise causes sweat to drip down Tom's forehead. "It's not real. You got to get this over with," he says.

Immediately, with a heavy foot, he steps on the gas. As the engine revs, the car's momentum shoots forward. The tires hit a significant bump, giving the impression that he has run something over. Looking straight ahead, Tom refuses to stop to check things out. "I'm not falling for that one," he says as he pushes the gas pedal to the floor. "It's your imagination, Tom. Drive. You got to drive."

The squeal of the tires from the added power resonates like the cries of his beloved animals, escalating his panic. He is spiraling, and all he can think of is that he needs to check on his pigs. In desperate need to free up his hands, he shifts his position to steer with his knees, then uses his free fingers to frantically rub the sides of his head to squelch the clamor.

"They only want to ruin things for you because they don't want to see you happy. Happy, that's right. This is what happiness looks like. You have never been happier," he says. Then, with a crazed look in his eyes, he neurotically forces a laugh. "Happy."

Thinking he sees something from the corner of his eye, he checks the driver's-side mirror.

Tom catches sight of a woman's silhouette by the barn. She's wearing a light-colored dress with a crinoline-lined knee-length skirt and is illuminated by the moonlight. Rather than upright, her stance is contorted, and her body is hunched as if broken.

Tom continues to drive with his foot heavy on the gas, even though something about the woman is so alluring that it makes it impossible for him to look away. His body leans closer to the mirror to get a better look, and his eyes narrow as he tries to make out the woman's face in the mirror's reflection. But, no matter how hard he tries to get a clear view, he cannot since her gaze is fixated on the ground.

Suddenly, the truck's tires hit a dirt mound. The unexpected bump shakes him from his stupor, and he over-adjusts the car's wheel, almost causing himself to crash. The unoiled axis sounds a heinous shriek as the car harshly swerves to correct.

The wind picks up, tussling the leaves of the overgrown brush and briars located ahead at the back of the property. Something about the swaying movement calls to him.

His vision jolts forward as he tries to navigate the dense vegetation. Unable to see through it, he turns his headlights on bright to help. Growing impatient, he presses harder against the gas pedal to speed up his drive to his destination.

A wave of exhaustion takes over his body, and, unable to fight it, his eyes begin to close. While drifting in and out of lucidity, he hears a woman's voice whisper in his ear. "I love you, Tom," she says.

The voice is familiar, and its comforting tone overwhelms him.

It's his mother.

Tom's face turns pale. "Momma?" he asks.

As his eyes spring open to scan the cab for her, he runs out of time to hit the brakes, and the front end of his car collides with Danny Boy's truck.

Upon impact, his forehead carries on with the momentum of the crash and forcefully collides with the unforgiving steering wheel, consuming his eyes with pure darkness.

Chapter Eleven
THE CIRCLE OF LIFE

The hard collision has left the truck's entire hood crumpled like a smashed beer can.

A slow stream of gasoline trickles from the punctured tank and seeps into the ground. Hours pass as the tank empties with no sign of movement from the vehicle's cab.

The morning sun rises, and a tiny woodpecker flies overhead. Making a delicate landing on the car's windshield, it pecks at the glass, then harshens its attempt when not seeing any results.

Tom's body remains slumped over the steering wheel in an involuntary deep sleep. Even though the blow to his head has forced him into an unconscious state, it's still the best slumber he has gotten in his entire life. His eyelids flutter as he slowly regains consciousness.

A woman's scream echoes from across the field. That, paired with the stench of gasoline, jars Tom awake.

Abruptly pushing himself off the steering wheel to sit upright, he picks up where he left off and immediately begins hyperventilating. "Momma?" he asks.

As he desperately tries to scan the cab for her, the quick movement of his eyes provokes a dull headache, and he clutches his skull to ease the pain. Swirling in a state of illusion, his lapsed memory keeps him from deciphering which of his recollections is accurate and how his current real-ity came to be.

The woodpecker continues tapping on the glass. Tom glances at the window to scare the bird away, and the orange sunrise blinds him. Attempting to fight what feels like a horrible brain freeze, he winces to stop the aching sensation from worsen-ing, but nothing changes.

In a panic about not being able to recall precisely how he got into the field, he wants fresh air to clear his mind and desperately fumbles with the door handle to let himself out. Tom pushes the door open with his shoulder and attempts to take a step, but his numb legs buckle beneath him. Unable to hold himself up, he falls face-first to the ground. He grabs for the foot railing of the mon-strous truck, and, while waiting for some feeling to return, he supports his weight on it to help him stand.

The scream of a woman echoes again in the distance.

Tom shudders in response to the shrill cry. He fights through the pain of his headache, trying his best to decipher whose voice is calling. The cry triggers memories of his childhood, and still thinking of the encounter with his mother, he believes it might be her calling for help.

Tom shifts every ounce of his focus to making his legs cooperate. Needing a little extra assistance, he leans forward, grabs the base of each thigh, and lifts them one at a time to maintain steady momentum. Dried mud covers his body like a suit of armor, and in his concussed state, the extra weight, though minimal, feels like he is lugging a ton of bricks. With every dragging step, the sun rises higher in the sky, and the birds sing to cheer him on.

As he makes his way out of the pasture, his muscles shake from fatigue, but the sunrise peeking over the top of the barn encourages him to push forward.

Noticing that someone has already opened the sliding barn door shifts his focus from the ringing in his ears, and he sees Claudia's red convertible parked outside.

As he trudges onward, Tom tries to brush the dried mud crumbles off his pants and put on a smile to make a good impression, but the crash's impact has caused a brief stint of facial paralysis.

Spotting him walking toward her, Claudia gets a discontented look in her eye, and she dramatically lowers her shoulders with a long huff to release her frustration. She bolts out of the barn to greet him. Tom attempts to pick up his pace and limps faster, ignoring the jabbing pains in his tingling limbs.

Claudia flails her arms in the air to get his attention, and the poofy skirt of her white flouncy dress gracefully compliments the chaos of her running legs. She shouts at the top of her lungs, "Where have you been?"

As she gets closer, she notices how dirty he is and scrutinizes the slight limp in his step while picking apart his appearance. His scuffed-up nature disgusts her, but rather than show an ounce of worry; she's irritated by his presence. Thinking he's out to ruin her day, she becomes snide. "Is this what bachelor parties look like nowadays? Huh?"

Tom's post-concussion mind doesn't intake her quick-firing questions. As he tries to process the overload of information, he becomes lost in his words and responds with stutters.

Having a moment of softness, Claudia realizes her behavior might scare him off before the wedding, and she quickly pulls back her negative energy. With a slight shrug, she stops her harsh approach, and her lips twitch as she forces a smile. "Well, what can I say? At least it's better than a stripper," she says.

Grabbing tightly around his arm, she attempts to speed up his walking pace. Tom tries to keep up.

Claudia playfully giggles. "Sorry for the little nervous bride outburst. It's just that I've been planning all night, and every chapel I spoke to had given me the same terrible news that they could not get us in for a couple of months. Can you imagine?" she says.

Taking a dramatic pause, she puffs out her chest proudly and carries on. "But then I had this brilliant idea. I looked at the newspaper as I was about to give up, and I gave one last phone call to this fellow who lives a little out of town. His name sounded familiar. I'm pretty sure a friend of a friend or something used him before as an officiant to get hitched. He only had one opening on his schedule, and surprise! That opening is today. He says the Lord told him to offer it for half the price, and he would even come to us!"

She glances at Tom's face and, noticing his lack of expression, clears her throat as she prepares to paint a picture for him. Then, with a coy chuckle, she waves her free hand toward the barn. "It will be perfect. Just us and the pigs. Can you imagine?"

The overload of information stuns Tom, and without saying a word, he nods.

Cutting in, Claudia takes that as confirmation and talks faster. "Lucky for you, I bought this dress a while ago for safekeeping and threw it on this morning, and now, here I am, all ready for our 'I do's,'" she says with a smile.

Her long-winded speech finishes as they make it to the barn opening. Feeling parched, Tom licks his dry, dusty lips to wet them.

Claudia pushes on his back to usher him inside the barn. "He should be here in an hour or so," she says, brushing off the mud chips from his back. Then, realizing the effort is futile, she latches onto his shoulder and forces him to turn to look directly into her eyes. Her speech slows to give him instructions. "That means you need to clean up the pigs. We can't have them looking like they are right now. We will have this memory forever, meaning it needs to be perfect. So, while you clean them up, I will head inside our house and pick out an outfit for you to wear for the ceremony. That way, we can kill two birds with one stone."

Not giving him any room to rebuttal, she twirls around and heads for the farmstead. Tom is speechless. As he watches her dance away, he can no longer keep it together, and his vision blurs. His hands clutch his temples to focus, and, slightly delirious, he steps outside to look for the coiled-up hose. Finding it around the corner of the barn, he stretches out the kinks, turns on the faucet, and staggers back inside with it dragging behind him.

The sight of the trailing water causes the pigs to squeal. Their high-pitched sounds add to the throbbing sensation in Tom's head. He tries to tune them out by keeping his focus locked on the fence's gate as he staggers toward it. Slowly opening the latch, he lets himself inside. Thrown off by the pen's disarray, he glances at the tipped-over water trough and, unable to remember the details of what has happened, heads over to refill it. Now barely able to stand upright, Tom alternates the hose's flow back and forth between filling the container and spraying the animals.

The pigs enjoy their light rain shower and scamper around the pen in circles.

As Tom notices he is nearly finished filling the trough, he watches Olive approaching and, turning the hose onto her, sprays off her fur. Her snout wiggles.

Confident he has gotten most of the mud off; Tom turns the hose toward himself to moisten his lips. His vision blurs. Feeling woozy, he recognizes something is wrong and places the back of his hand against his forehead to feel for a high temperature. Not sensing that he's running hot, he pulls his fingers away and notices them covered with blood. His feet wobble beneath him in response, and his sight gives out.

As his body falls to the ground, the hose's erratic movement catches the pigs' attention, and they anxiously move around the pen, fearing that its serpent-like motions mean it's a snake.

Tom lays in the mud, face up and non-respondent. Deep down in his skull, something has been brewing like a cup of coffee. Little does he know that the head trauma from the steering wheel has caused a brain hemorrhage. It has continued trickling through the previous night and the current morning, like the gasoline from the wrecked car. The violent impact has set his fate in stone.

In hopes he can find comfort in the animal's noises, Tom tries to listen to his surroundings and, having no vision left, calmly attempts to tap into his other senses.

He tries to swallow, but his throat won't cooperate, and, functioning by the book for once in his life, he falls into a seizure. As he commences his last moments on earth, he knows his mother was right all along: he will soon join her, and the thought of having a genuine connection of human companionship provides him the solace to succumb.

In unison, the pigs hear Tom's last coughing gasp, and their beady eyes shift toward his body to observe. Drool forms on their lips as they release snorts that sound like slow-building applause and, smelling fresh blood, wait for their new ringleader, Olive, to give instructions.

Olive, unaware of what is going on, is conflicted by Tom's odd behavior. His body is limp, and she can't decipher what's happening to the man who has always provided her with the necessities of life. With naive confusion, she rushes to his side to check on him, and as her foot graces his shoulder, she gets a waft of something in the air—the same iron stench the others had been smelling—and her stomach rumbles. As her nose frenziedly wiggles, her eyes turn crazed. Unable to pinpoint where it is coming from, she lets her snout guide her toward the food, and her moist nose presses into the gash on Tom's forehead.

Overruling her emotion, her hunger takes over, and she cannot differentiate the meal in front of her from any other. Without Tom's identity registering in her mind, she loudly squeals at the others to alert them that it's breakfast time.

All at once, they flock to join her, and, taking their place around Tom's corpse, they circle up like a stampede of hungry predators. Skipping a moment of silence, they don't see it necessary to give thanks but immediately start using their dull teeth to fillet him.

At first, they are cordial and take turns, or try to, but the taste is sweet, like nothing they have ever had before, and the pigs instantly become ravenous beasts. They can't quench their tastebuds fast enough and bite at one another, fighting for his blood. Running out of flesh, they crunch through each of his bones like candy canes, devouring every bite quicker than the last.

When they have eaten down to the mud, they are still not fully satisfied and want more. Overtaken by their addiction, they rabidly sift through the dirt to find any morsels that have been overlooked.

Olive, still hungry, notices a single eyeball that has rolled away and playfully lunges toward it. Pinning it against the corner of the wall, she stares directly into the center of its clouded pupil and hesitates. As she analyzes the darkened orb, something about its look touches her soul; it's familiar to her.

It brings back a sense of fond memories, triggering a wave of compassion through her heart, and her tear ducts swell.

Lowering her nose to the floor, she gently nudges the sticky sphere and, using her snout, rolls it toward her mouth for her tongue to gently scoop it up. Not understanding the cause of her reaction, she lets it sit between her teeth for a moment, and then, giving one subtle oink, she chews.

Meanwhile, the herd realizes that every scrap of Tom's corpse is gone, provoking a revolt, and the scene rapidly escalates out of control. In a dehydrated rage, and with a slew of shrieks, they charge the water trough, each hoping to be the first to overtake it. Impatient for turns to get a drink, they prop their feet on the edges of the trough, and the rocking of their weight tilts the water container over.

As the gallons of water flood the pen, it sweeps over the area where Tom's body once was, and any remaining evidence of his corpse is washed away. All the crimson-stained dirt is darkened and blends into the mud.

The newly formed pool of dense sludge subdues the pigs' hostility, and their short attention spans flip from ire to excitement. They chase each other, belly-sliding through the mire while playfully nudging at one another as if to play a game of tag. Olive, hearing their happy oinks, turns around to observe. Not in the mood to join, she silently watches them roll around as they cover their bodies with an additional layer of wet filth.

Each exuberant squeal distracts from the sound of a car turning into the farmstead's driveway, and the slow approach of the wheels seems to fly under their instinctual radar. The large, new model truck has a crew cab; its custom bed slightly extends past the dual back wheels, which were added for pulling trailers and hauling farm equipment.

As the sun hits the red-orange paint, it glistens, and the sparkles reflect onto the tinted windows. The snail's pace of the driver selecting where to park shows that they have never previously set foot on the property. They circle the yard several times before stopping near the barn. The driver takes their time getting out, remaining in the vehicle for several minutes while the engine purrs.

Claudia impatiently peers out through the living room's first-floor picture window. When she initially entered the house, she'd presumed the task of choosing Tom's wedding clothes would take longer, thinking he would have several options to pick from, but she finished the job rather quickly, discovering that he only owned one outfit suitable for a marriage ceremony.

She intentionally delays returning to the barn, fearing that going outside too soon will force her to help clean the pigs. So, she bides time by digging through Tom's family's belongings. Finally, after not finding anything interesting, she sits in front of the bay window, waiting for the officiant to arrive.

Even though she had pictured the man facilitating their matrimony to be driving something a little more luxurious, she knew it was him since they expected no other company. Putting judgment aside, she makes the most of the situation and runs outside to greet the parked car.

The vehicle's engine stutters as it shuts off. Claudia notices the driver's side door open. She picks up her pace, yelling to get his attention and clutching Tom's dress clothes underneath her armpit. Her facial expression is over the top with excitement as she exuberantly waves to greet him. "Hello! Hello, there! Even though you are early, I take it you must be the gentleman I spoke to on the phone, who's going to be beginning the happiest moment of a young couple's life," she says.

The young man, wearing a fashionable pair of driving gloves, only catches the beginning of her long introduction as he exits the vehicle and waves to acknowledge her. He takes a moment to straighten the material of his checkered navy suit with thin, argyle orange accents. After ensuring that every wrinkle is gone from his tall, lanky body, his hand brushes a chunk of his dark-brown chestnut-highlighted hair from his youthful face. As he tilts his head to look at her, his perfectly sunken, stubble-covered cheeks and chiseled jawline reveal his age as roughly thirty years old.

With a nervous smirk, his shyness translates through his coy demeanor. "Yup, sure am. I'm your guy," he says. He extends a hand and waits for her to shake it. "I'm Samuel."

Not expecting a young—or, for that matter, attractive—man, Claudia fights to keep her jaw from dropping open as she moves even faster toward him. She tries with all her might not to blush or exude her flirtatious personality while sensually posed near the truck. Her grip around Tom's clothes stiffens as she pretends not to be out of breath while accepting the man's greeting.

Their hands clasp, and she can't help but admire the touch of her fingertips against his supple leather gloves. Knowing how expensive they must be, she grins from ear to ear. To her, their luxurious nature makes up for him driving a truck. "It is so nice to meet you. I adore your way with fashion," she says.

She catches herself getting carried away and, not wanting to cross any boundaries, retracts her hand while clearing her throat. "My name is Claudia." Then, as she fishes for a compliment, she twists, flouncing the ruffled petticoat underneath the dress. "The bride-to-be."

Samuel's eyes widen after glimpsing her thigh. "Well, aren't you a sight for sore eyes?" he says.

For Claudia, the exchange feels like love at first sight. She can't help but wonder why she hasn't seen him around town before. Wanting to get answers, she turns on her manipulative charm. "So...

if I remember correctly, your ad in the local paper mentioned that you're new in town? I'm usually pretty good with faces, so I'm sure it's true because I know yours is one I would not forget," she says. She gives him a shy glance and bats her false eyelashes so rapidly that the flutter looks like a flapping blackbird's wings.

Thrown off by the question, Samuel anxiously smiles and takes a slow approach to tell his story while gauging her reactions. "I wanted a change of scenery to escape the fast-paced life of big city living, so I moved out here not too long ago. I'm about the age to settle down and have a few kiddos, and the idea of being closer to family was appealing," he says.

Noticing how she perks up at the mention of children, he smiles. "This is a great place to raise kids."

Claudia nervously fidgets as she eyes his overabundance of superb genetics. She has always favored having a backup plan, and with him being a picture-perfect candidate, she cannot help but flirtatiously inquire further. "You want kids?" she asks with a charming giggle. She realizes her question may have sounded too forward, and her cheeks blush. Then, still wanting the information, she takes a more passive route. "I can't imagine it would be hard for someone like you to find a nice girl."

A bead of sweat forms on Samuel's brow. "That's mighty nice of you to say. Ever since my parents separated when I was young, they did not leave me with a great example of what to look for in a relationship," he says. He breaks eye contact and looks to the ground as he squeezes the back of his neck and chuckles. "It's a funny story. That's-that's the reason I got ordained. When my mom found someone new to marry, she dreamed of having me be the officiant, so here I am. With the change of scenery from the big city and all, I can only hope things will turn around for me in the love department."

His eloquent speech immediately infatuates Claudia, and with his puppy-dog eyes, she knows his personality would be malleable in a relationship. She bites her lip and, wanting to seal the deal, gives him her best sultry look. Suddenly, his large truck doesn't look so bad to her, and she finds the notion of them choosing similar paint colors destiny.

Samuel wants to finish what he came to do and switches topics. He motions to the wad of clothing underneath Claudia's arm. "I take it that's for the groom?" he says.

His pointed words snap her daydreaming mind back to reality, and she reluctantly looks down to address his remark. "Yep. These are for my husband-to-be," she says. Seeing that Tom's suit's color scheme is like Samuel's, she nervously adjusts the clothes underneath her arm to hide the odd likeness, then gestures to his attire. "Looks like you have similar tastes."

Even though Samuel sees no equivalence, he chuckles and plays along. "What can I say? It's a great color combination," he says with a shrug.

They smirk as they stare at each other in silence. Then, as their exchange becomes awkwardly stagnant, they make their way to the barn.

Meanwhile, Olive remains waiting in the same spot as earlier, convinced that her beloved Tom will miraculously reappear inside the barn's tin walls. Her eyes dart to every little noise to see if it's him, and, having been at it for a while, she realizes he may not return.

At the very moment she feels defeat, she hears Samuel's laugh, and thinking it could be Tom, her ears perk up, and she loudly lets out a squeal of excitement to inform the others. All the pigs cry at the top of their lungs.

Samuel and Claudia are standing just outside the barn's entrance, and the clamor makes her wince. She anxiously laughs to cover her disdain. "I guess we'd better get in there. Those cheery little voices should mean that my fiancé is just about done cleaning up the pigs for the ceremony."

Samuel smiles from ear to ear, feeling different from Claudia about the animals' noise. The sounds bring him comfort, and, though drawn to their calls, he refrains from pushing past Claudia to get a peek at the herd and waits for her to lead the way.

Claudia has no desire to go inside, but he appears attracted to her feigned interest, so she continues with the charade. She fights back her flirtatious smirk as she spins toward the barn and waves for him to follow.

Olive hears their footsteps against the concrete and, lifting her head, sees the silhouette of a man built similarly to Tom. She runs to the fence and presses her snout between the bars.

As they approach the pen, Claudia hears running water, and the sight of the grimy pigs wipes the cheery smile from her face. Trying to keep her composure in front of her guest, she solidifies her smile by clenching her teeth. Not seeing Tom in the pen, she calls for him. "Tom, dear, our officiant is here," she says.

Her pupils shift to look at the sight of the unchaperoned hose and the flooding inside the barn. She is livid even before her eyes can survey the full extent of the mud-soaked pigs.

Feeling herself losing control, she turns away from Samuel, and as she pretends to search for Tom, the clothes from underneath her arm tumble to the ground.

Samuel's similar stature to Tom continues to pique Olive's interest, and, still thinking it's him, she squeals to get his attention. As Samuel scans the herd, he answers Olive with a huge grin and wiggles his fingers in a wave.

The added noise of the squeals sets Claudia over the edge. Not knowing what to do and seeing no sign of Tom, she nervously paces to bide time. Ignoring everything happening around her, she glances at the open barn door and wonders where he could be. Finally, she concludes that he must be somewhere outside, and she uses the running hose as an excuse to look. "If you would just excuse me for a quick second?" she says.

Breaking his gaze from Olive, Samuel turns toward Claudia to reply. "Would you rather I just come back at a later time?"

Claudia doesn't take kindly to his offer, thinking he's trying to ruin her chance for matrimony. Her biggest fear is remaining single for life. She rushes faster to the open barn door, shouting over her shoulder, "Nope, that won't be necessary! I will be right back. This is typical; he is just forgetful sometimes. I need to go shut off the water."

Samuel purses his lips and gives an awkward nod. "Sure thing," he says. As he waits for Claudia to return, he makes his way over to Olive. Squatting to her level, he stares deep into her eyes. Samuel continues to observe the herd, and the blatant signs of dehydration and malnourishment trigger concerns about the pigs' health.

Claudia shuts off the water, and with her mission complete, she quickly tries to fix her disheveled hair before running back inside. She laughs loudly to get Samuel's attention away from Olive. "That's better," she says.

Samuel's gaze doesn't break. The sight of his gentle nature with Olive causes her to stop, and without uttering a word, she quietly backs up to stand in the doorframe. As she admires the interaction, she grins at the thought of Samuel fathering her children. "I hope you know you are in the presence of greatness. That's Olive, the winner of our local pig jamboree," she says.

Samuel smiles as he removes one of his gloves and reaches through the fence to rub between Olive's ears. "I remember seeing that precious little snout all over the local paper," he says. Then, tickling her under the chin, he laughs. "Who's a little star?"

Olive's eyes light up. Something about his voice soothes her, and she leans into his affection. Then, Oinking, she nudges his fingers to scratch the side of her head. The pig's behavior causes Samuel to chuckle.

Immediately, the interaction reminds Claudia that she still must find Tom, and with Samuel distracted, she seizes the opportunity. She clears her throat to get his attention. "I got an idea: Why don't I let you two get acquainted before the ceremony while I round up the man of the hour?" she says. Then, pausing, she tries to maintain her composure while waiting for a response.

Samuel smiles at Olive. "Of course. You know where to find me," he says. His laughter mirrors her soft oinks.

As he finishes his statement, Claudia has already scanned the vicinity of the barn's interior, and not finding any clues regarding Tom's whereabouts; she falls back on her original assumption that he's somewhere outside. Spotting his wedding outfit lying on the floor, she grabs it as she passes by.

Claudia steps through the door while shielding her eyes from the sunlight. She holds up Tom's suit and gives it a good shake. "Good as new," she says. Then, standing in front of the barn, she scans from left to right. "Momma always said there's a good chance a man will get cold feet and run away on their wedding day, but she never said where to find them."

The breeze churns up a small cloud of dirt from the ground, forming a dust devil that scares a flock of birds chirping in a nearby tree. Claudia knows there is nowhere in the open to hide, and, not seeing him anywhere, she calls out, "Tom!"

She pauses, waiting for a response, but only hears her voice echo back, and her heart races. Her eyes glance to the field of tall grass in the distance, then to the short ivory heels on her feet. "These shoes were meant for walking, but not over the top of that crap."

The sun's intense heat is causing her makeup to run, and she looks at the cloudless sky with disdain. The flock of birds chased from the tree circles and squawks overhead. Thinking they are mocking her dilemma, she glares at them with contempt, and something splashes on her shoulder. Claudia already knows what it is. She refrains from looking immediately, and a shiver of disgust runs through her body. "Momma told me that's supposed to be good luck," she says.

As her rage builds, she quickly retreats into the shade cast by the barn's overhanging roof, looks to the farmstead's window, and then to the field across the way again. "There's no way he's out there. I would have seen him from the house if he had gone out into the wilderness. I had a direct view." Discouraged and prepared to give up, she rests her hands on her hips.

Claudia is convinced that this hell on her wedding day must be directly related to karmic debt for something she has done in her past. Not wanting to create any more bad luck for herself, she forces a smile on her face and waves goodbye to the flock. "Have a great day," she says as they fly away.

As soon as she can no longer see them, she refocuses on finding Tom. She scans the barnyard again and still sees no sign of him. It stumps her.

Tom is nowhere to be found.

Sweaty and disappointed, Claudia gives up and heads back into the barn. In her mind, each step is a walk of shame, and wallowing in her failure, she sprawls out onto the barn's concrete floor to sob. She doesn't know what is worse: that she was dumped by someone far beneath her in looks and personality or that her makeup is ruined.

Unaware of what has occurred, Samuel pulls his hand away from Olive and promptly puts his glove back on. Springing to his feet, he rushes to Claudia's side to comfort her. Not knowing how to help, he thinks of a generic response. "There, there. Everything will be ok," he says.

His sympathy causes a flood of tears to stream down Claudia's face. The worst of the worst has happened. An attractive stranger is forced to exude pity for her, making her feel pathetic. Her head burrows further into her hands, hoping to escape the shame.

All she can picture is how people will treat her differently when they find out Tom, of all people, stood her up at the altar. After publicly rubbing her relationship with Tom in the mayor's face, she knows he will be a catalyst for her social demise. Thinking of the horror, she cannot bear being the town's laughingstock. The only thing she cares more about than getting hitched is others' perceptions.

Even though Samuel has just met Claudia, and her hysterics make him uncomfortable, he wants to get to the bottom of the problem and lightly places his hand on her back to show support.

Claudia releases a chain of snorts as her cries turn into an ugly wail, and she worries how horrid her makeup must look after the salty tears have had their way with it. She channels her anger, fixating on how Tom is purposely ruining her life. Having never genuinely known the man, she isn't upset over him missing, but rather, her humiliation and the idea of there not being many eligible bachelors left in town to marry.

Claudia refrains from looking up, strategically hiding her face, knowing she must bide time to adequately build her victim narrative. She lets out a mournful wail. "He's gone," she says.

The sound of her agony ramping up causes the pen of pigs to join in, and, trying to match her cries, they loudly squeal. Unable to process what's going on over the commotion, Samuel assists her with standing and leads her somewhere quieter. As he escorts her to the exit, he becomes tired of her dramatically flopping body, so he guides her to take a seat on the end of the concrete slab underneath the sliding door frame.

He kneels on the ground next to her to provide a few encouraging words. "Okay, just take a few deep breaths," he says.

While pretending to hyperventilate, Claudia peeks through her fingers to see if he's buying it. Pleased by his engagement, she loudly bellows and continues with the waterworks. "You wouldn't understand," she says.

Placing a hand lightly on her knee, Samuel attempts to help by continuing to engage her in conversation. "Try me," he says.

Even though she would prefer to play a different role, Claudia knows she must come across as vulnerable. She lifts her head slightly and looks into his eyes, showcasing the state of her tear-streaked makeup. Her vanity aches as she dramatically plays the part of the jilted fiancée. "He beats me," she says. Not having thought far enough ahead to develop the storyline, she doesn't know what to say next and, sniffling, hides her head in her hands to think.

Claudia stares at the ground between her feet as she lifts her trembling hand and points over her shoulder into the barn. "He beats all of us and severely neglects them and me. That's why they are in such a sorry state. He hates us, but I couldn't bring myself to leave. You have to understand that those pigs are like family to me. Being a woman who's always wanted children, my instinct is to protect them as if I were their momma. They are all I've got. I can't leave them. I just can't." As she ends her rambling, her cry escalates.

Lucky for her, the story hits a soft spot in Samuel, and his jaw briefly clenches with anger. From a young age, he had watched his father abuse his mother and even dealt with the violent repercussions firsthand. Yet, never having been old enough to do anything for his mother, he feels like now could be his chance for redemption.

Overtaken with the desire to save the damsel in distress, he springs to his feet and pushes up his sleeves. "I'm going to find him. Don't worry; I'll take care of it. I'll give him a taste of his own medicine. Men like that don't deserve to breathe," he says.

The sound of his will to fight for her makes Claudia fall for him even more, and her heartbeat quickens. Everything about the presentation of his masculine demeanor turns her on. The last thing she wants is for her storyline to be put in a position where holes can be poked in the narrative. She wants the situation with Tom behind her so she can move on.

With a gasp, she grabs Samuel's pant leg to seal the deal. "Please, you will only make things worse," she says. She wipes the invisible tears underneath her eyes, releasing a few theatrical sniffles and quivering her lip. "Maybe you were just sent by God to save me. Let's leave it at that."

Samuel stops to look at her and notices the inconsistencies. Even though he thinks the response is peculiar, he softens his expression to show compassion. "Maybe," he says, extending a hand to help her up from the ground. "At least let me get both you and the herd somewhere safe. If something happened to you now, I would feel mighty guilty."

Claudia timidly takes his hand and stands to her feet. Remembering a tendency, Tom exhibited that she thought was cute; she attempts to mirror his bashful expression. She looks off into the distance toward his truck and stammers. "I-I couldn't live with myself if I dragged you into this mess. I-I mean, if something happened to you... I... I...," she says.

The addition of her overdone stutter throws Samuel off, and he tries to recall if she'd had it before. He comforts her by lightly touching the tips of his soft, leather-gloved fingers to her chin and slowly turning her head to look into his eyes. "Don't worry, your pretty little head. You are safe with me. I have plenty of extra room at my place, and you are welcome to stay with me until you are back on your feet," he says.

The disappointment of not receiving a marriage proposal from her performance of a lifetime sets in, and she feels cheated. Believing that she has not done enough to attain her goals, she wobbles on her feet and, acting weak, looks at the ground as if she is about to faint. "But what will your wife think?" she asks. Then, sheepishly, she places her head back in her hands.

Shifting his expression, Samuel feels awkward and, tired of the theatrics, gives a vague answer. "Doesn't exist," he says. He focuses on the rescue mission and pushes past her into the barn.

Claudia steps outside, away from view, and smiles ear to ear while performing a quiet happy dance. Once out of her system, she reminds herself she's supposed to be sad and reactivates a quivering lip.

She is ready to begin her new life and becomes impatient. Confused about what's taking so long, Claudia sticks her head inside the barn and catches Samuel gathering pig-related items. "What are you doing with that crap?" she asks.

Samuel continues with what he is doing and shouts back over his shoulder, "What do you mean? We got to get your kids. I have a small pasture at my place. I will load them up so you can all be together."

Claudia stops dead in her tracks, irritated at herself for stupidly adding them to her narrative at the height of the emotional charade. Never having liked the beasts, she wants to leave them behind, and as she waits outside, unable to control her frustration any longer, she exposes her true intent. "You had to bring them into the storyline, didn't you? You had it in the bag. Momma always said that less is more," she says, stomping her feet and rolling her eyes.

Hearing her shift in disposition, Samuel, out of curiosity, pops his head out of the barn to witness the truth.

Trying to recover the facade, Claudia spots his face and enacts a one-eighty to her demeanor, instantly pretending to cry. "I can't leave them," she says as she feigns, wiping a tear from her cheek. "I'm sorry I'm emotional. That is the sweetest thing anyone has ever done for me. I just needed a moment to ask God what I did to deserve such an angel."

It's too late; the gig is up. Samuel is unmoved by her performance, and being better at the game, he effortlessly keeps his composure. Without as much as a glance, he passes by her as he walks toward his pickup. "I'm going to move the truck a little closer to load the herd. Okay? You don't have to lift a finger. All you have to do is stay put right where you are and keep lookin' pretty," he says.

As Claudia watches his pace shift to a jog, she sighs. She's in love.

Samuel hops in the cab, turns the key in the ignition, and revs the engine. He takes a moment to prepare, ensuring there is no blind spot and adjusting his rearview mirror. He places his foot on the clutch and peers at Claudia's smug face in the mirror's reflection. They make eye contact, and he smiles.

Claudia coyly grins back, and, feeling on cloud nine, she fantasizes about their future, kids, house, dog, and all.

Without breaking his gaze, Samuel reaches forward, grabs the stick shift, and throws the truck in reverse. Then, as he continues to focus on Claudia in the review mirror, he puts the pedal to the metal, and his eyes turn a shade of cold black as the vehicle picks up speed, spewing gravel and dust as they race in her direction.

Not processing what's happening, Claudia, still in her daydream, doesn't have time to move, let alone scream, before her body is pulled underneath the enormous wheels.

The sensation of the tires clearing her body makes Samuel smile. "The only thing I dislike more than a heartless bitch is a conniving one," he says. Then, switching the car between drive and reverse, he laughs as he continually plows her over.

When he is confident she is dead, the act loses its luster. Samuel places the vehicle in neutral and lets out a howl of excitement. He fumbles for the glove compartment and, upon opening it, spots the corner of a photo sticking out from a pile of feed receipts. He carefully takes it out to look at it.

The old black-and-white picture has a slight yellow hue, and even though it's worn from the combination of age and sun exposure, it still perfectly paints a surreal scene of the rolling hills of a large pig farm. Two men, confidently standing side by side, are surrounded by hundreds of pigs, freely roaming, with long coats of hair matching Olive's. Apart from the color of their work coveralls, they appear pretty similar. Both are in their late teens, medium stature, with dark hair and pieces of hay hanging from their lips. The top corner of the picture reads *1928, Kentucky*. Beneath each of the boys are their respective names: *Ernie* and *Earl.*

Samuel lightly places his fingertip on the silhouette of the boy labeled Ernie. "I wish you were still here to see this, Grandpop. I told you I wouldn't let them get away with stealing our pigs. It took me a little longer than expected to find them, but I am finally bringing our kinfolk home," he says.

He glances up, reveling in his years of commitment and hard work finally paying off. Then, shaking his head, he chuckles. "All it took was a local newspaper headline about an unusual pig with hair and a little town gossip."

Still, in disbelief, he laughs again. "Most real pig farmers outside this Podunk place know what Mangalica pigs are. Shit, we're the biggest breeder in the USA and only one state away. Such a sense of self-importance, people always wanting to think they discovered the next big thing to add to their town's welcome sign."

A bird happily chirps as it perches on top of the barn. The melodic tune makes Samuel grin. Ready to get back out on the road, he leaves the engine running and quickly jumps out of the cab. He makes his way to the back of the truck and opens the tailgate, ignoring the sight of Claudia's mangled body. As he assesses the bed's available space, he feels a rush of excitement. "Well, it may be a little cramped, but we must make do."

The animals squeal as he begins to head inside to gather the cloister of pigs. Samuel takes a moment to look at them, and he can't help feeling an overwhelming sadness as he approaches the pen. Knowing that lack of nutrients can dictate the quality of their coat, he imagines the horrific suffering all but one must have experienced to become bald. "Don't you worry. You will have your full coats of hair back soon enough—just in time for winter."

The pitch of their squeals switches to excitement as he loads them into the truck's bed and latches the back. He hops into the cab, edges the truck forward, and then gets out one last time to hose off the blood from the vehicle's underside. Once finished, he does a careful once-over and returns the hose to its original spot.

As he climbs into the driver's seat, he is filled with a sense of peace, knowing that he has kept the promise to his grandfather.

Taking each of his leather gloves off one by one, Samuel looks at the golden wedding band on his finger, then places the balled-up leather in the center console. "Time to go home," he says.

Looking in the rearview mirror, he makes eye contact with Olive and, with a grin, begins his long drive home.

BOWIE

About Author

Gitte Tamar

Brigitte, "Gitte," Tamar was born in a small rural Oregon town. Growing up, she was enthralled by scary tales featuring poetic tones and consistently gravitated towards writing darkened narratives. In the different storylines, Brigitte explores the harsh realities of social issues faced by today's generations. This includes the dark outcomes brought on by peer pressure, addiction, homelessness, mental illness, childhood trauma, and abuse. She feels it is essential to share narratives that refrain from sugarcoating the topics society tends to shy away from.